My Dinner with Andrea

My Dinner with Andrea

Jen Durbent

ISBN: 978-1-948743-00-6

My Dinner with Andrea

Publication: 1.0-print (First Edition), 2018.

HYBRID Ink, LLC
Independent Publishers of Thoughtful Writing

hybrid.ink
Everett, WA

Printed in the United States of America
10 9 8 7 6 5 4 3 2 1

To All My Sisters.

Content Warnings   Violence; the ruination of literature by inclusion of content warnings; attempted rape; references to problematic works; t-slur; racism; polyamory; disability and ableism; Nazis; sex; death; ACAB; gore; and acknowledging the terrible, horrible, no good possibility of happy queer people.

Part I

"Because that is a beautiful fucking story, told flawlessly."

— Callen Lebo

Chapter 1

"Faith?" came the voice behind her; she rose and looked at Andrea. Andrea, another tall girl—even taller than usual—visibly trans in a "fuck you" kind of way. *So pretty.* If she had Andrea's transition timeline, Faith would look at it on the Internet and just cry over it, her own dysphoria sucking out hope.

"Andrea?"

"Hello!"

"Nice to see you again," Andrea said, looking Faith up and down. "You look so cute!"

Faith looked down at herself. She looked at her fat self. She looked down at her own lopsided tits and skirt and all that.

"Thanks," she said, trying not to sound sarcastic. "You're cute, too. Uhh, take a seat," she gestured in the general direction of another chair.

If Faith was honest, she had been hoping Andrea wouldn't show; she would be left alone at a dinner table with a bill, three empty drinks, and a good 'stood-up story' to share on the Internet and with her wife. Mostly the Internet, again, if she were honest.

But here she was. And here was Faith. Two trans women on a date. And Faith had no idea what to do.

Faith watched Andrea take her seat. She wondered if she should have risen and pushed in the chair. She would have done that before of course, when she looked like a man. Chivalry was what she was 'supposed' to do. She felt by not getting up and pushing in her date's chair, she had fucked up the whole date, and they were still at "Hello."

"So, thank you," Faith said, "For coming out to see me again. After the coffee thing I wasn't sure, but I reached out and..." she let herself trail off.

"...and here I am." Andrea finished after a half-tick. Her voice was nice and passable to Faith. Faith instantly thought about her own. Andrea had heard Faith's voice before—when they met over coffee—so Faith tried to convince herself everything was okay, Andrea accepted the date, after all. Faith only succeeded slightly.

"So...have you been here before?"

"No. Have you?"

"No."

"Living dangerously, aren't we?" Andrea asked.

"Well I like spicy food. This seemed a good choice."

"Spicy is good. *Tacos rule*," Andrea said in an affected voice. If it was an impression, Faith couldn't place it, so she just nodded.

Andrea looked at Faith. "You don't get it...It's okay. It's a movie."

They looked over the menus in silence.

"Oooh, queso dip?!" Faith said, betraying her internal promise to take it easy tonight.

"Yum! Let's."

"Yes."

Faith held the menu a little farther away than seemed reasonable. *Was she far-sighted?* Andrea wondered. *How old is she? She looks, like, 30, tops.* One part of her mind said to another, *Estrogen.* and—with great effort—stopped hypothesizing.

"How spicy do you like it?" Andrea asked.

"Very." Faith said, trying not to read innuendo into it and failing. Andrea giggled.

"Yeah, I figured we'd get along." Andrea said looking over the top edge of the menu, hiding a grin. "Okay, I know what I want. You?"

"Yeah. I think chicken tacos."

"Good choice. I'm going with the *quesadilla grande*, whatever that is."

"Cool." Faith said, then thought: *Why did I say that?*

They put their menus down.

"So," Faith started, "what do you do?" She paused for effect, then continued. "Not for a job. What do you love to do?"

"Oooh, good one." Andrea sat and bit her thumb with her front teeth. "Yeah, so...I write bots."

"Bots?"

"They're silly little social media creatures. I make them. They say things periodically. Respond to people. They use simple decision trees and grammar to generate plausible sentences."

"That's...that's clever." Faith replied. "I never heard of that before."

"Yeah. It picks at, for want of a better word, the right places in my brain. The language, the coding, the logic, fucking with people," Andrea laughed. "It's just a hobby. I have maybe three or four. They take some time to work through the logic and vocabulary."

The waiter approached. They ordered drinks (no alcohol), appetizers, and their entrée.

"So how about you?" Andrea asked.

"Excuse me?"

"You asked me what I loved to do. How about you?"

"Oh. I'm pretty dull. I...I play a lot of Destiny."

"That shooter-slash-loot game?"

"Yeah."

"Cool." Andrea said, and smiled in a way that almost said she meant it. "Why do you like that?"

"Because I seem to be good at it. I get to meet people and do activities, get loot and so on."

"Neat. What does your wife think of it?"

"Oh, she hates it." Faith said. She laughed. "She groans every time I start it up, but she lets me have it."

Andrea gave her a raised eyebrow, "Lets?"

"Well, it's not a permission thing it's a, 'well, that's what she does' thing."

"Uh-huh."

They sat quietly for what felt like minutes, but was maybe ten seconds. Faith messed with a napkin.

"She knows about me, right?" Andrea asked.

"Oh. Yes," Faith said. "Hold on. I'll show you." She took out her phone and opened a photo.

In the photo was another woman, she was holding a sign saying, "Hi, Andrea, this is Faith's wife, Michelle" and it had the date.

"Well that's pretty weird."

"You asked for it. We kind of figured it would happen. I sometimes over-prepare."

Andrea laughed.

"I've thought it through a lot," Faith said. "This is...this is actually my first date since I...since I transitioned—besides with my wife. We still do the dinner and a movie and the like"

"Really?"

"Really." Faith said. "My wife is straight; I no longer do much for her there. But we still love and care for each other, so she dates men and I date who I like and...well, you're the first." She didn't finish the sentence, which should have included, "who didn't stand me up."

They sat in place for a minute, Andrea kind of unsure what to say.

"No pressure," Faith injected and laughed.

"Yeah..." now it was Andrea's turn to be insecure, because this is what happens here: Both women are keenly aware of who they are and what they are doing and who they are and are with and suddenly it all seems more real. Is the person at the next table staring? [Yes.] Is the bathroom a single occupancy? [Thankfully, also yes.] Does the waiter care? [Only in the benevolent *happy for them* way; his father transitioned when the waiter was young.] All these things and other things like them come up in their heads.

"I'm really not hungry," Andrea said.

"Me, either. But we already ordered."

"We'll get it to go. Be a good lunch tomorrow. You wanna come to my place and play video games?"

"Sure." Faith said, maybe a little too fast, but she wanted so much to be out of there.

"I've got an NES and frozen pizzas." Andrea forwarded, "I mean, if the take-out sucks."

"Well why are we waiting?"

$$%^&*(

On the Nintendo, Mario and Luigi were triumphant, of course. The princess was saved. The pizza was eaten. Andrea was asleep on her couch. It was not even 10:00 PM.

Faith looked about. She got up and started walking around, quietly judging Andrea's place before she went to the bathroom.

It was a loft. View of the river, over a chocolatier. This would be an extravagant place in many other cities, but less so here. The loft was partitioned with furniture and floor coverings, a single bathroom the exception. Faith headed towards it. She always peed in safe spaces before leaving. At this point, it was a habit.

As she walked by a bookshelf, she scanned some of the spines. Some cookbooks. A smattering of sci-fi and horror books. A handful of linguistics books and some on programming (the three-monitored monstrosity on the other side of the kitchen was probably where Andrea worked, Faith figured). The bookshelf had the same trans books Faith had. Mock. Auntie Kate. She laughed when she saw Nevada.

After peeing, she collected her purse and looked back at Andrea, still on the couch. Faith put her purse down, took a blanket from the bed, then brought it to the couch and put it on top of Andrea. A small smile came to the sleeping lady's face.

Faith left, careful to lock the bottom lock of the door as she did so. She then made her way to her car and home.

$#^%&(*(&%*^^&%^&*(

One of the perks of living in a small city is it's possible to transverse the whole thing in minutes if one knows how. Faith pulled into her driveway 10 minutes after she locked Andrea's door.

Her wife was still awake. On the front of the house was a set of wooden planks with both their names engraved. Faith's plank bore significantly fewer signs of weathering than Michelle's.

"Hi, honey." Michelle said as Faith made her way in. She was sitting in her recliner watching television.

"Oh hey. I thought William was coming over?"

"Not William. Adam. He was supposed to but his work came up."

"Ahh."

Faith approached and kissed her wife chastely.

"How was your date?"

"Weird."

"What, she showed up?"

"Yeah. She did. And she's so pretty." Faith said.

"I'm glad she showed," Michelle said and smiled, "it's about time one didn't flake out."

"Yeah."

"I need a shower. Can you help me? You can tell me about it while I'm in there."

"Sure. Crutches or chair?"

"Crutches today. I've been sitting all day and I can't feel my ass."

Faith smirked and shook her head. That was the joke. *Of course,* she couldn't feel it. Paralyzed from the waist down. That was the joke. Get it?

She broke her back a long time ago, but in the years since she'd taught herself to walk—in a manner— with crutches, swinging and using her legs as...well, a third leg. It was not a graceful act, but it did the job.

Faith retrieved the crutches and gave them to her wife, then got the shower started.

Once Michelle was settled in the shower chair she used (she hated being *in* the tub, the dirty water disgusted her), Faith sat next to her in a chair outside the tub.

"So, we were gonna go to Fiesta Reales."

"I never been there."

"Neither had we, but after we ordered our entrees we decided we weren't hungry for Mexican." She didn't tell her wife about the insecurity Faith and Andrea had felt. It was easier. Michelle would probably insist they were imagining it. They might have been, partially, but not all the way.

"Oh."

"Yeah, so we had them box the order and took them back to her house. Loft actually."

"Did you bring me some?" Michelle teased.

"No, dear. I actually left it in her fridge now thinking on it."

"Oh. So, did you eat?"

"Yeah; frozen pizza."

"Hell of a date night."

"We played video games."

Michelle laughed. "Fucking nerd. God damn."

"Shut up. It was fun."

"Did you two fuck?"

"Michelle!" Faith said, her mock outrage carrying over the white noise of the shower. "I'm offended."

"Oh, fuck off, bitch. It's barely 10:30 so I bet you didn't."

"Yeah, no. She fell asleep on the couch."

"Kiss?"

"No."

Michelle moved the shower curtain aside and looked at her wife.

"You want to fuck me?"

"Of course."

"Well, sorry."

"I know."

"I'm sorry you didn't get laid."

"Well it wasn't just for that. It was nice to hang out with her."

"How so?"

"She just...didn't seem...like...I don't know."

"Out with it."

"She was trans and I was trans but we really didn't talk about it. I think it's just...something we're dealing with, but it wasn't at the forefront tonight. It was cool to just hang out with someone and play video games with no expectations or educating or explaining or justifications. Just total acceptance. It was so nice. Then she fell asleep next to me on her couch."

"So like a trans friend."

"Yeah."

"But she's cute."

"Heck yeah." Faith said.

"Can you get my back?" Michelle asked. Faith stood to do so, her knees popping. "Are you going to see her again?"

Faith took a moment. "I don't know. I'd like to, but maybe I fucked up and she won't want to see me."

"Maybe. But she fell asleep next to you," Michelle said. "At least she was comfortable enough for that."

"Yeah."

Faith went to change the subject: "Did you have fun with the creep yesterday?"

"Alan?"

"Is there another?"

"He is a little weird but he's nice so far."

"I don't trust him."

"Noted."

Faith continued to wash her wife. She did one leg followed by the other, slowly taking time to clean her feet and inspect for any wounds she wouldn't feel. This was the routine.

Michelle looked down on her diligent wife, who was getting wet from the shower. Faith did not complain, doing the thing she had promised to do so many years ago with love and care.

"Hey, Faith," Michelle said.

"Yes?"

"I love you."

"I love you, too."

"We're still not fucking."

Faith shook her head, "Of course. But I'm still gonna use the vibrator."

Chapter 2

The next morning—over coffee at her place—Marc looked at Andrea, "So, wait. I'm your token straight white male friend?"

Andrea looked at Marc, "It appears that way."

"That's weird."

"Why?"

"Because most dudes are straight and white."

"You only think because you see yourself as the default. But we queers stick together, man. My friends are mostly queer because I feel safer around them. So you should be honored I even deigned to have lunch with you later today. I even still have my dinner from last night from that taco joint."

"Oh yeah, your date." which was the whole reason he was there at this terrible hour, a physical check-in. Andrea was pretty paranoid. She'd had experiences.

"Yeah, my date." she said. "Why do you gotta make it sound like that?"

"Like what?"

"Like it's not a real date."

"Sorry."

"Yeah, yeah." Andrea waved him off.

"How was it?"

"Fine. She was a little shy. We decided to leave the place; it was giving us creepy vibes."

"How do you figure?"

"Can you stop for a minute? Fucking Christ. Everything you ask is 'How did you know?' I just did. So did she. Ever since I transitioned you've been subtly undermining me."

"Sorry." he said, but he wasn't.

"Fuck that noise. Just listen. Being an ally is so easy: shut up when we talk, speak up when someone else is saying shit and we're not there. That is all. Fuck, boy." She shook her head and waved everything away. "Anyway, yeah, we just brought the food home and baked a Tombstone. We played Mario. It was nice."

"Seems kind of unexciting."

"I wasn't looking for exciting last night."

"Bummer." he said.

"Perv. Anyway, I must have passed out; I fell asleep on the couch but woke up with a blanket over me."

"Aww," he said.

"I know, right? She must have put it on me before she left."

"Pretty nice of her."

"Yeah."

"How did you meet her?"

"OKCupid. She's married"

"Really?" he said. "So, you're the bit on the side." He presumed. Because that's what he'd done to girls like her, because of who he was.

"No. The wife knows I exist. She showed me a picture on her phone, like with my name and a 'hi' and the date and shit."

"That's weird."

"I dunno. Thoughtful." Andrea said.

They looked at each other. The bowl he had packed sat idle and unlit on her coffee table.

"Not feeling it today." she said, waving her hand at it.

"Your loss." he said. "You mind if I do though?"

"Have at it."

She watched him light the bowl.

"So," he said, holding it in, then re-breathing a little. "You think anything will come of it?" He let out the smoke, hacked a few times and listened.

"I don't know. I've never dated a person with a wife."

"Well," he started, trailing off.

"That was different. Not open like this," she said. "and you didn't fucking tell me until later, anyway, asshole."

He laughed. "The divorce was almost final anyway."

"Whatever. I know I stopped dating men for a reason."

"What's that?"

"Trans dykes are good and pure," she said and smiled at him, quoting some meme she read on the Internet not long before.

"Whatever."

&%^*&(

Andrea was working at her desk (as Faith figured), when Faith sent her another message. This one popped up on one of the virtual machines running remotely due to Faith's aforementioned paranoia.

"Had a good time yeste4rday. Would like to see you again and I don't want to waste time with BS 'will she text me' so I'm doing it. Anyway. Whatever the answer thanks hope to hear from you soon."

Andrea looked at the screen.

"Sure. Friday. This time I'll pick you up. Just need a time and address."

Sent.

Back to work.

^*&((&&^%&$^#*%^()&*_(_

Faith cried with joy when she got the message, weeping softly in the bathroom at work. She heard the door open and someone walk in and then walk out. She was pretty sure it was one of the prudish women who thought she was an abomination or something. Didn't matter.

Days would go by without talking to people, even at work.

But now someone wanted to be near her. To be with her even if it was for an evening and over some food, which she guessed she was now traditionally required to pay for (given she asked Andrea), but even still.

Faith went back to her office, closed the door, sat in her chair and let the feeling wash over her.

She had a date.

She smiled and closed her eyes. Tears dried under the florescent lights.

Chapter 3

Faith looked at the clothes in her closet. They were perfectly serviceable, but plain. Designed more for a work day than a date. She was still new at this and she hadn't accumulated anything of note. Especially no two things that went together.

"Michelle?" she called. There was no answer. Was Faith home alone? She was. Michelle had a date. Some guy. Even his name had slipped Faith's mind. Andy? No...Alan. Yes Alan was it.

"Shit."

She had to figure this out herself.

She kept picking up the same 3 pieces and putting them back. Some garish white top. Some t-shirt, and a skirt. She didn't know where they were going. She gave a long eye to the dress in the closet.

"I should just wear something I'd wear to work." she said. She found her favorite skirt in the hamper. It didn't smell, but someone had put a wet towel on top of it. And by *someone* Faith realized that someone was Faith.

Her phone buzzed; she picked it up. It was Andrea "I know we agreed 8 but I'll be there ~8:15. Can explain when I get there. Sorry."

"That's fine. See you soon," Faith responded. She sighed out loud. This meant she had an hour instead of 45 minutes to figure out what she was going to do. She didn't know if it would help.

She strained her eyes to look at the dress in the closet. She bought when she was still in the closet too. "Is that green or red?" She couldn't remember. Michelle had told her once months ago when they were going through things for the season.

She picked up her phone and opened the app she used for such things.

"Red. Okay. Got it."

She looked down at the shoe collection. She picked out the black ones. She thought about stockings. What about the ones with the line up the back? What were they called? Didn't matter. She hadn't worn those in months, so they were probably in the drawer with the rest of her socks and such.

Her heart beat faster. Sweat at the brow. Fuck.

Okay.

Okay.

She threw the dress on the bed and shoes on the floor, and approached the dresser. Her stuff was in the bottom drawer and top. Michelle had the middle for accessibility. Faith didn't see them right away so she dug some more, the occasional sock popping out and onto the floor while she rummaged.

She found them. Perfect. Wound in the tight little ball she left them in after the last time they were washed.

She unrolled them, inspected for runs, not noticing the one across the butt.

Bra. Underwear. Top drawer. Faith had, like, three bras, all sports. The one nicer one she'd had went missing some months ago and she hadn't been able to find it. She looked through Michelle's drawer a few times but it wasn't there, either so Faith gave up. She wore the second nicest sports bra and hoped the dress wouldn't show the straps.

She assembled herself. Bra. Panties. Breast forms she used as a shield. Sometimes she would bounce them in her hands when misgendered, as if to say "hey! did you *see* these?"

Many months ago, before she got dressed and showed herself for the first time to her family, she felt like she would choke on the terror. She felt it would absorb her. The cliché "lump in her throat" was meaningless before then. Who would get *that* nervous? Then she learned. And she was enlightened, or something.

She felt the lump thing right now.

Then it was something else.

She saw herself from the outside then. Her body going through the motions. Of course, this was all metaphorical. But her body seemed act of its own accord. It was like during her last eye exam and they did one of those tests and the image splits and things were separated. She tried to bring herself back into alignment with her, well, self. There was a struggle and she saw her own hands hesitate to roll on the stockings (pantyhose, really, if she felt technical, which she did not). Then her perceptions rolled into place, asserting themselves once again over reality. When she finally could think about what she was doing she noticed the heel of one of the hose sides was on top of her foot.

"Fuck," she unrolled it and turned the whole thing over and started the process again. Was this disassociation? A mini fugue-state? She didn't know. It just was something that happened.

She looked at the clock. There was very little time to spare.

The lump faded and she went through familiar motions, letting her body do the things it knew how. She trusted it and tried to not interrupt it, just pretend she was going to work.

%^&*

Andrea pulled into the driveway. When she opened the door she noticed a piece of garbage had rolled out from under the passenger seat onto the floor of the front seat. She threw it on the floor of the back seat.

Despite the awkwardness before, Faith was nice. Was there something off about her? No? She thought about it. There was something off about everyone, Andrea decided. For one, Andrea slept with an old stuffed animal. It was the last thing her mother gave to her. After she came out to her parents, her dad kicked her out. A few days later, a small package came in the mail; she could identify her mother's handwriting anywhere, and the address label was no exception.

She opened the box from her—Andrea supposed "estranged" was the word people used—mom. It was one of those build-a-bears.

The clothes in pink and purple and white. No note. Just the cheesy birth certificate they give you. The name on the bear: Andrea; the birthday: her birthday, some decades before.

But she would just be a trans girl with a trans flag colored Care Bear. What was that? Was that right? Not morally but rational? It was not the way so-called mature people or whatever behaved or conducted or whatever the word was. But consider: a teddy bear? Of course, she also knew a 40 year old cis man with a collection of the things. So, was maturity actually normal?

Gut check: how do people conduct themselves in this kind of thing? A quote floated in and out of her mind: no rules of architecture for a castle in the clouds. But for her this was unprecedented mostly because such things like this romance didn't exist, really. Did they? Sure she had friends who had them but she never actually met those people in proverbial flesh. They all lived on the coasts and this was certainly not the coast.

And how many stories could she read about this?

Shit, was it even a romance yet? One and a one-half dates. There wasn't even a kiss, really. But there was something. A feeling, like the first breath after coma.

Faith, this woman she barely knew, fucking tucked her in on the couch? Such a kind gesture. What is it when the world is large and mean and vast and empty of meaning that these tiny things could grow? Those thoughts were something Faith probably didn't even put much thought into, but when Andrea woke up warm and comfortable on her own couch she knew Faith had taken a second and worried about her comfort. Even one gesture, one act, was far nicer than many people had been to her as of late.

She still held onto her friendships, even if they were painful. She hung onto them because she didn't know when someone else will come by. She hung onto them because she felt so so damn lucky someone even put up with her freak self, even here, just as friends.

Andrea breathed heavy.

She thought about her bear.

She thought about the bottle of Xanax in her purse.

She thought about reaching in her purse and putting 2 of the little tablets in her mouth and washing it down quickly with the old soda sitting in the cup that had been in her car for 2 days because goddamn Xanax taste super gross. She decided she should do just that.

Dear reader, don't worry. This isn't a story about drugs. This is not foreshadowing of some great dark thing about anxiety. This is just normal. This is just how some people deal.

Two pills popped in, downed a swig of old, flat pop, the door handle pulled, step out, walked up the ramp (not registering what that implied), knocked, waited for the door to open.

Faith opened the door.

$%^*&(UI)

Faith looked at herself in the mirror and tried not to panic.

The bottom of the dress was too high, the neckline too low, the waist was too tight, and her boobs weren't big enough to fill out the cups in the dress.

"How did this fit for work?"

"It didn't," Michelle's voice came to her from memory.

"Fuck."

She was going to be here any minute. At least her eyeliner...was not on. Or mascara.

"Fuck."

Eyeliner is a tricky beast. It can befuddle the most patient person, and typically it cannot be hurried, especially at first when one is still learning how best to keep one eye closed while you do odd contortions.

But occasionally, the Trans Goddess smiles upon you. The eyeliner goes on perfectly. The wrinkly skin on the outer corner of Faith's left eye is slightly less wrinkly today and it does not cause the eyeliner pen she's using to skip across its surface. She doesn't bother with wings because she doesn't have time, really. The other side...and it matches. Holy fuck! Praise the goddess!

Mascara on top, she finishes the slight dusting of her bottom lashes just as Andrea pulls in.

She keeps her eyes open to let the makeup dry. So she looks at herself in the mirror more.

"This will have to do."

She picked up her phone snapped a picture to send to Michelle. Before she sends it she sees an unread message from her.

"Love you. Have fun. I won't be home tonight. Don't worry. House is yours, if you need it."

"Thank you. You too. Love you, too." She attached the photo and ran downstairs to answer the door; Andrea knocked.

When Faith opened the door on Andrea she immediately thought she overdressed, but then she looked closer. Was that a suit? A smart one.

"Hello!" Andrea said. "You look amazing."

"Hi! You do too! Nice to see you again. Did you want to come in for a minute or are you ready to go?"

"I can be ready," Andrea said and looked down on an imaginary watch, "Now." A smile; one of those big stupid grins. "You just look amazing. Wow."

Faith looked down and tried to see what the other woman was seeing. "Thank you," she managed.

"Okay. I'll drive."

#$%^&*(&^%#

"Really?" Andrea said. Faith looked at her, looking for signs she did something wrong.

"Sorry."

"No that's fine. I'm sorry."

"I hate my body," Faith said. Meaning more than the allergy, they both knew. Andrea decided not to head down that path, yet.

"Oh, that's nothing you could have helped. I should have asked. Shellfish allergy. Got it."

"It would be worth chancing to order something not seafood, but I don't have an EpiPen. Need to save up for one."

"That's fine. Burger?"

"Burgers are good."

Andrea waited a second. "So how did you figure out the shellfish thing?"

"I ate it...I almost died," Faith said flatly.

Pause. Andrea wondered what the fuck she did.

Faith laughed. "Sorry. I just thought it was funny," she said. Laughed again. "I was like eight. I got some good grades for the first time in a long time. My mom says I can choose a place to go to dinner for a treat. So, I picked Red Lobster, and I have no idea why. Commercials probably. So, we get there and I'm chowing on the cheddar biscuits and order some shrimp dish. I don't even really process what it is when I get it I just chow it down, again. I eat like four or five of them and then suddenly one of the biscuits gets stuck in my throat. So, I go into anaphylactic shock and I'm choking on those damned biscuits. Thankfully someone—I still get cards from him—realizes at least one of the problems and does the Heimlich on me. Which gets the biscuit out, shoots it into my 7-Up, knocking it over and spilling it. But as everyone is happy the biscuit is out of my mouth and cleaning up the mess, I'm still choking. The busboy, who is cleaning up the soda, sees me gasping for air and before anyone can stop him, he drags me onto the ground, lays me flat, whips out his own EpiPen, and jabs me in the leg. A few seconds pass and I can breathe again. That bus boy, saved my life. Guillermo."

They were pulling into the lot of the burger joint as the story was concluding. Andrea said. "Hell of a story."

"Yeah. So. No shellfish."

"No shellfish. Got it."

After the entrees were ordered, and they sat across from one another.

"I never tried Sushi, though."

"Kind of like sucking a guy's dick." Andrea said, "I mean, I did a few times. But they were just kind of gross. I thought maybe if I try it, I might like it? But no."

"I agree. Kind of slimy and weird."

They laughed.

"Well, only if you order something like eel. I mean even the salmon or tuna, which is supposedly good, was just kind of ick. I think I could take a spring roll."

"Oh, sure. That sounds nice. I mean, I like the rice and veggies. Just the meat, ya know?"

"For sure."

They munched on some peanuts on the table. Faith ate them whole. Andrea shelled them.

"That's weird," Andrea said.

"Yeah. They say that. But I like the salt."

Andrea tried it. The extra salt on the outside of the shell was perfect, "Oh. Oh yes."

"Good, ain't it?"

"Yes."

"Don't eat too many or you'll not have any fun in the bathroom tomorrow," Faith said.

"Gross."

"Yeah. For sure."

Faith tossed one more in her mouth, and then started shelling the next.

"You know," Faith started then stopped. What to say? Like, she was okay with the silence. One can't be married for more than a decade without occasionally being quiet next to another human.

"Yes?"

"I have no idea what to do here. I'm just kind of lost. I think I said this last time."

"Something like that."

"I haven't dated in a long time. If ever, really. And, ya know?"

"It's okay. I know, I read your profile." Andrea looked at Faith and saw something in her eye. It might have been a tear. It was hard to tell because it wasn't big or wet, it just was...wet. It could be anything. "It's okay. What are you thinking?"

"Do you want to know?"

"Would I have asked if not?"

A sigh. "You met my wife?"

"Ahh, she lays those verbal traps?"

"She does sometimes. She doesn't mean to but she does. Well, she means to. But I don't think of her as bad. Just everyone has their thing, ya know?"

"They do," Andrea said. Tried to remember her thing. Succeeded in finding several things. Put them aside. Tried to. For now.

Faith sighed. A long one. She closed her eyes.

"I love Michelle. But I am not sure where I stand with her any more. Not being into women. And I've not been touched in months. Maybe a year. It's just…just…this feels right. Even if you and I don't get along—and I hope we do—this is the relationship I wanted. Two women together."

Andrea nodded. "I read on the tweet machine once: 'I like girls, but in a gay way.' Something like that?"

"Yeah. Precisely that."

"Same. I tried to date ladies before I really went full time. And guys after. Because ya know, heteronormative-ness and all," Andrea said, waving her hand. "And there's pluses there, not many though. Dudes just felt wrong. I was forcing myself. When I went back to ladies I felt rightness. And trans women especially so."

"Really?"

"Yeah. I mean. Cis women can be good. And some enbies are amazing. But…there's something about another trans girl. Some unspoken stuff. We don't have to educate a cis person all the time, don't have to be watching out for their feelings when we get angry at our own bodies or some gendered shit they hadn't thought of or noticed. I had a friend who was having a baby. I tried to be there for her and I just felt so much dysphoria. I started…well…yeah it was bad."

Faith nodded.

"I just want babies. Ya know?"

Faith put her hand across the table, touched Andrea's hand. She was surprised by the softness of it. At her own hand's softness, as well.

Andrea looked up and smiled at her.

"I couldn't go to her baby shower or anything for like the last two months of her pregnancy. I haven't seen her at all since the baby. I am happy for her but I just...reminds me of what I am and what I can't do. I even muted her on Facebook. It goes deep. "

Faith nodded again. "I get it."

"Yeah."

The waiter came and they pulled their hands apart from one another's.

"I'll check on you in a little bit," the waiter said and walked away, leaving empty drinks un-refilled.

&*()(*&^%^&*(

"I had fun with you tonight," Andrea said to Faith as she walked Faith up to her doorstep, both of them arms akimbo, unsure if one should touch the other.

"I did, too."

"Do you want to go out again some time?"

"Yes," Faith said, and Faith thought it was maybe a little too enthusiastically. But Andrea smiled big, calming Faith.

"Yes. Me too."

They reached the door, the porch light pushing their shadows out long and tall into the night.

They turned toward one another.

"So. My wife isn't home," Faith said. "She's out with her boyfriend, Alan."

Andrea nodded. "Honey. I would love to, but tomorrow I have to drive into Chicago early," she said. "It's a long day."

Faith sighed, obviously disappointed. Andrea's worry lines appeared.

"I'm sorry."

"It's okay. I don't know how this goes. I've read way too much erotica."

They laughed.

"Next Thursday," Andrea offered. "I am free in a couple Fridays after, too. There's a show at a club and I know the band; I got an invite and a plus-one."

"I will make it happen," Faith said.

They dropped their arms.

"May I kiss you?" one of them asked. It might have been Faith. It might have been Andrea. But both wanted to.

"Yes," said the other.

They took one another's hands and leaned into each other. Their kiss was just a moment. A single precious moment.

Kisses may be magical, but kisses may also be pure. It was not a kiss for ages, it was a kiss for them, for that moment. It was enough.

Faith stumbled back giggled and fumbled with her keys and unlocked the door. Andrea stepped away to give her room to open the door.

"Have a good night, Faith."

"You too, Andrea."

"Thursday?"

"Thursday."

Chapter 4

Faith woke up, hung over, as Michelle came into their bedroom.

"Wakey wakey, sleepyhead," she said. She slapped Faith on the ass.

Faith made some unintelligible noise.

"You have a good night?"

"Yes," Faith said into the pillow.

"Good. You work today?"

"No."

"Okay. I might need help later."

"Yeah."

"Sorry about your head," she said. She knew somehow. "I should have realized when I saw the bottle in the kitchen trash."

"S'okay," the face in the pillow said.

"We'll talk later. I'll leave some ibuprofen out."

"'kay."

"Faith?" Michelle said before she left the room.

"Yeah."

"Love you, Faith."

"Love you too, dear."

$$%^&*(*%&

The drive from Rockford to Chicago is best made a metaphor of going to the bathroom. Rockford driving is as if it were an empty bladder; things go on sometimes and it's okay. There is not a lot of pressure and only the typical every day life-and-death risk people take on while driving.

As one approaches Chicago, it ratchets up.

The pressure starts noticeably increasing as one passes Elgin, a larger exurb of the city. This is the "I should go to the bathroom but I will wait for the commercial" level. Then, once one hits the Woodfield Mall (whatever city that's in) the pressure is very high but manageable, as if it were near the end of a very long movie.

Then when one turns off any other road into Chicago itself, it's like there is a cat who decided to jump right on your lower abdomen. The pressure increases exponentially until you reach your destination, culminating in the final crushing "will I hold it" feeling of finding a parking space.

Andrea pulled up to Vannah's apartment complex. She lived a little off Lake Shore, so a nice area, not far from Boy's Town, where the street signs were painted with rainbows and the crosswalks were the same, where pride marched every year, growing slowly less political and more corporate as the years rolled on. As capitalism marches queer folk toward assimilation, the quislings are granted their "rights." It's not right but that's how things seemed to go.

Still feeling pressure, Andrea looked for a spot she could poach so she can run upstairs to pee. She was afraid to pee in public restrooms. She would if she had to. There was even an app on her phone to help her find friendly ones. It's far more useful here in Chicago. In Rockford, she was the one who tagged most of them. She still avoided unknown ones if she could.

She found one and ran to her friend's door, then knocked, brief hug, and ran to the bathroom. Vannah knew the drill.

Vannah and Andrea both have appointments at the clinic. STI screening and hormone level checks. Vannah's STI is more important to her; Andrea hasn't gotten laid since her last one. She's doing it in solidarity with her friend and trans sister, who just started seeing a new guy.

"*Fuck!*" Andrea yelled through the bathroom door while peeing.

"There's no reason why this should feel this good."

"If they knew how good peeing felt for us when we finally can they would never pass those bathroom bills," Vannah offered as she changed in her room out of her pajamas.

When she got out she hugged Vannah again and more properly this time. "Good to see you."

"Good to see you."

"You ready for this?"

"Yeah. I mean, I am pretty sure I'm clean. Only hooked up with one guy since the last one. But getting with James, ya know."

"Eh, one is more than me."

"Sorry. I get it. Thanks for coming with me for this," Vannah said.

"Sure. Love you."

"Same to you, girl." Vannah said that a lot. "*Girl.*" It was a verbal tic, Andrea kind of figured it as. But it was an affirming one. It would probably be weird if she adopted it. Her being white and all.

"I want to move to injections," Andrea said. "They seem easier."

"They are. Less times to remember. Though remembering every two weeks is tough. I just made a reminder on my phone." Vannah laughed. "I remember when I first went to injections. I told myself I would never forget. But I did."

"Yeah, I thought that with the pills, so we'll see."

"Anyway. You parked in a safe spot? Don't want you towed or anything while we're on the El."

"Yeah," she said. "I hope so."

"Okay."

^&*$&^&(*(

"You seeing anyone?" Vannah asked while the Red Line poked underground for a minute.

"Yeah. Kinda. We just started. Like, third date last night. Or second. Ya know, coffee."

Vannah rolled her eyes and shook her head. "Whatever. And?"

"She's nice. I like her. She invited me in last night."

"She. Okay. And?"

"I demurred. I had to come see you today," Andrea said.

Vannah laughed. "You fucking white girls."

"What? We're responsible," Andrea grinned at Vannah. "One of us gotta be. I got up at like 6 today to drive in here for you. I get here and you're still in your jammies"

"True, true." Vannah laughed. "But would you have?"

"Yeah. I mean we haven't talked about sex yet."

The El poked its head out into sunlight. Slowed. A stop. Not theirs.

Vannah nodded. "Talking is important."

"And I'd be her first."

"Like she's a virgin?"

"Nah, like her first trans girl. She's married."

"What?"

Andrea sighed. "It's fine. Her wife is straight. Now they're poly because they love each other but...fucking, ya know?"

"Gotcha."

"Anyhow. She's cute."

"Yeah?"

"She's white. Chubby, but I like that."

"It can be cute on the right woman. The chubby thing; I don't know about being white," Vannah said and laughed.

"Cute. But I like her. What about your new guy?"

"Oh. James is nice. Ya know. Never dated a trans girl before. Like, I have to teach him all this shit. But he treats me right. He doesn't hide when we go out. He takes me to dinner and takes me home. Ya know?" Andrea nodded. Vannah, as gorgeous as she was, was often not treated well. She was hidden away to be a piece on the side. "I met his mom. So, I mean, I'm ready to marry the man at this point. Even if he's coming 2 minutes in."

They laughed, both thankful they are the only ones in the subway car now.

There was an automated tone through the intercom. "This stop: Sheridan," the computer said. They stood.

%^&*(%&$*%&(

Swab. Pee. Blood. In and out in a half hour for both.

"Thanks for doing that with me."

"Yeah. I should ask Faith—"

"Faith?"

"Oh that's her name. The girl."

"Oh, shit. That name. LOL," Vannah literally said LOL. "Anyway, if she likes it whatever."

"Yeah, I mean she didn't watch as much Wheel of Fortune when she was a kid as you."

"Fuck. Savage. Savage."

"Yeah, I got you."

"I was a spelling bee champion. You know?" Vannah said.

"Yeah, I know. I was there. You beat me."

"Damn right I did."

Pause.

"So now what?"

"Now we fucking get tacos, girl."

Andrea nodded.

Fucking tacos. Fucking A.

$%^*&(*(&^*%$

Vannah hugged her friend tight. "You be good now. Drive safe. Text me when you get home. Not when you're down the street. When you're in your apartment or condo or whatever with the door locked and everything."

"Okay. Will do."

"She's not bothering you anymore?"

"Denise? No. She hasn't called me in months. I didn't even change my number."

"I told you, girl. She was bad news."

"I know you did."

"I don't trust her."

"You trust me, don't you?"

"I do. But I am not worried about you. I hatched you, my little egg."

Andrea looked right into Vannah's face and held her hands as if to promise her everlasting soul, "I know. She's not around. It's okay."

"Andrea," Vannah said, squeezed Andrea's hands. "She said she would kill you. Girls like us, we must be on guard. She'll get away with it too. Crazy cis fucker."

"I know. I'm careful," Andrea said. She leaned in and kissed Vannah on the cheek. "At least she's not a fucking Nazi. That one guy. Shit."

"You dodged that one, girl. For sure," she laughed. "I love you."

"I love you."

Chapter 5

Michelle woke up Faith,

"Hey, honey. Uhh. I need you to look at something?"

"Wait what? What time is it?"

"3:30. I can't sleep and I need you to look at this sore. Is it infected? I can't feel it."

This happened every few weeks. There was a sore on part of her body Michelle couldn't feel and so she needed Faith to look at it. Faith was colorblind, making this a trifle bit hit-and-miss.

"Yeah. Yeah. Okay," Faith said.

Michelle turned on her side and showed Faith the sore in question. It looked puss-filled and unpleasant.

"You need a better cushion for your chair. You've been using it more lately. How did you notice this?"

"The usual. Self-inspection."

"Yeah there's something here. It looks gross but I don't see any signs of infection. I'll get the ointment."

"Okay. Thanks."

"Yup."

Faith walked into the bathroom and looked under the sink for the antibiotic ointment they kept for just such occasions and a small gauze square.

After dressing the wound, Faith said, "Did Andy see this?"

"Alan."

"Didn't Alan see this?"

"No. We...we didn't do anything."

"Why is that?"

"I don't know. I just…I didn't feel comfortable with him."

"But you've fucked him before."

"No. Not yet. I…I don't know."

There was quiet for a minute.

"Sorry."

"It's okay. You're a good woman."

"Thank you, dear. But I learned from the best," Faith said and kissed her wife on the cheek chastely.

"You're too good for me."

"If I was too good I would still be a boy and just like this."

"Don't." Michelle started. "You know I had a hard time. But I know I never said it wasn't because you were not good. You are good. You're just you. And I am me. And we're together. And I still love you.

Faith shrugged. "Was that it, dear?"

"Yeah," Michelle said, rolling her eyes, giving up for the night.

"Good night, dear. I love you."

"Love you, too."

$&(*)_*&^%$^

When Faith got up, Michelle had already gone to work. Her wheelchair was pushed off to the side. Just like any given Tuesday.

She walked as if she were tripod: her legs and crutches alternating, suggesting a kind of robot. Faith wondered how she did it when Michelle first showed her. It was their first date.

"I just kind of swing. I have to trust my legs won't buckle so I try to keep them straight. It helps me be more independent. I don't need a chair all the time. I can move about. I can drive, even; I just need the brake and gas controls where I can reach them. Also it helps so I don't get sores. I can't feel the sores. I have to check my legs and ass regularly to make sure there is nothing weird going on. It's a pain in the…well…I don't remember what a pain in the ass feels like. But it would be one."

Andrea had texted Faith. "We still on for Thursday?"

"For sure."

A second later, "Cool! See you 7 then."

Faith grinned.

"Meet at your place?" Faith asked.

"YAS!!!!!!"

%$&(*%^&*()

That night Faith played Destiny. It was a shooting game. It was kind of mindless, which is why she liked it. It was mindless in a way that engaged all of her active brain but also let it idle. It was a game that could be played by rote and without thought, especially when one only played against the computer.

As she watched her character go through some gate or pick up an orb or shoot the head of some low level alien, knowing they would show up again in 10 minutes, she thought about things. Because that's what she did.

Sometimes Faith thought about being trans or bills or wife or work—which she skipped today—but this evening she thought about Andrea. Because they had another date in a couple days and it was worth her brain cycles, she thought.

She didn't actually actively think about Andrea. She let her mind work through it.

What was the goal, here, with Andrea? To get laid? Andrea kept reaching out to Faith and responding when Faith reached out to her (which she admitted to herself she should have done more of), so she presumed Andrea liked her enough to spend time with her. But also she didn't want to scare her.

Why did Andrea want to spend time with Faith? Faith's insecurity kicked in. She kind of wondered if Michelle had paid Andrea. There were signs. I mean, mostly involving Faith feeling as if she was hideous and ugly and unworthy of even the slightest amount of attention. Nobody wanted a fat tran like her. What was she offering? A half-relationship? The love of a person who hates themselves. Who would want that? Hadn't she been told over and over she had to love herself first? So why bother?

And she didn't. Love herself, that is. She hated herself. She utterly detested herself. When she imagined dying (because she imagined it often) she imagined it in a crowded wood or rain forest, a violent sudden death, her corpse allowed to have some importance as it fed a few critters unfortunate enough to taste her flesh. Because what fun isn't suicidal ideation if it doesn't include vivid images of one's own demise.

In her game, she killed a big boss, a baron or other some such creature. The monster disintegrated and screamed as the virtual life ran out of him (her? Them?). The end of level credits showed. She had the most kills in her group of three. She got no rewards. The game immediately put her in another cavern to fight slightly different monsters this time. Those died from gut shots.

Should she cancel the date with Andrea? I mean she'd just be disappointed with Faith anyway. Better to prevent it.

She died at the hands of a crowd of low-level enemies. She put the game controller on her stomach and waited for resurrection, if it came.

As she waited, she looked at her stomach and imagined carving bits of it off as if it were a turkey. Sculpting it. Molding it. She tried to let the thoughts go and knew she would never have *that* shape. The hourglass. This body and its unfortunate rotundness was her source of dysphoria. She often wondered what if she could fix it. But she was smart enough to know even if she could fix that, there would be something else. Her voice, most likely.

Nobody wanted her. Even her own wife wouldn't touch her anymore.

Eventually the game's resurrection timer went off and she was fighting again.

She wondered if her ugliness was a true fact of the universe. And she felt it was incontrovertible. I mean, look at the evidence: her very body. And as it changed even that woman, who she had held and more over the years, decided not to touch her. Was she making a mistake? Was she really the terrible, ugly thing she now felt? Nobody touched her and all she really wanted in a way was that. To be wanted. Even if it was hollow, at least she would be of some kind of use, ya know? Instead she was treated like a medic and even then a poorly compensated one, with a peck on the cheek. But it was not all tit for tat; there was love there. A love with contentment and comfort in merely existing with another person and knowing they will always be there and care even if it was different now.

The hugs she got from her wife: Faith holds them far a little long because she knew it might not happen again for a while.

"Is this what a leper feels?" Faith mouthed to no-one. Of course, being trans isn't a disease, but she still worried about it because she's not a perfect pinnacle of prudence.

She died again. In the game. Not in real life or whatever her world was. That would be too weird. This was happening too much. After this level, Faith decided, she was done for the night.

She looked over at her wife, who was on the couch, playing some game on her own tablet.

I still love her. I still need her. So long as she is here.

She finished the level, but just barely. This time the lowest score of any of her compatriots. She turned off the game. Got up and went to her couch and laid next to her wife. Michelle stroked Faith's hair without really looking as Faith's eyes teared up and leaked and dripped on Michelle's legs, a gentle cry at such simple and inconsequential touch. Michelle's paralyzed thighs did not know tears ran down them, and Faith certainly was not telling anyone at all.

%&^&*()

Michelle woke Faith early again on Thursday, though this time she was polite enough to wait until just before the alarm was going to wake her.

"Faith. Faith. Can you check that sore again?"

"Yeah. Yeah."

Faith did and it looked worse than last time.

"Fuck. Infected still. We should hit the doctor this morning during her open hours."

"Okay."

Faith rolled out of bed. Her alarm went off. She killed it for the day.

All things being equal, being woken by your wife is nicer than an alarm, even if it was a few minutes early.

$%&^*()I_*&^%

"It's a pretty severe infection," the doctor says. Her voice low and clearly enunciating the goings on. The small exam room was relatively clean.

They were stuck in this city mostly because of the doctor. Adams had tried an experimental treatment. It could restore some operation of Michelle's legs. It had showed promise in animal studies but when Michelle had the procedure, its effects were temporary. She cried when she could feel her legs for the first time in a decade. She wiggled her toes. Masturbated. They had sex (because Faith hadn't transitioned yet). Then a few weeks later, it was back to how it was before. There was more crying. But Dr. Adams kept taking care of her, not charging the co-pays and other such things, even.

"And?"

"Well we'll treat with antibiotics. We'll culture it and see what it is, too, of course. We hope it isn't c-diff or staph or anything but one never knows. It was okay a couple days ago?"

"Tuesday. Looked like any other bedsore."

"Hmm. Quite quick." She breathed out heavily, thinking. "Yeah, I think that's what we'll do. I mean, I'll have to take a culture—"

"I won't feel it."

"Nope, and we'll see how it goes. Give you a shot of wide spectrum antibiotics."

Michelle made a noise.

"Yeah. I know. Digestive issues. It'll just have to be something we keep an eye on. Just...stay near a toilet, I guess."

"I had a date tonight," Michelle said.

"As did I."

"Yeah...you're doing that poly thing, right?" the doc said, not really a question. "That reminds me I did run the STI panels as you asked and you're clean. Both of you. I'll remind Adrian to have a copy for you for when you go."

"Okay," Faith said.

"But we each have our own massive biome on our skin. Who knows what this other fellow has on his skin. So...I mean, I would avoid him touching the area or really anything else until we get this cleared up and get you healed up. No reason to add yet another possible infection."

"Okay," Michelle said.

"Okay." Doctor Adams rose. She was tall and Faith felt a touch of dysphoria as she looked at this woman in front of her. She pushed it down. "So the nurse will administer the antibiotics—they're an injection—and she'll do it again in a week. Got it?"

"Yeah."

"Okay."

"Oh, and Faith?"

"Yes?"

"You look really nice today," the Doctor said.

"Thanks," Faith said. She was unsure of what the doctor meant, but she tried to take the complement as genuine.

The doctor left and they were alone in the exam room.

"Do you want me to stay home tonight?"

"Honey. We've both been planning these dates for a while now. I know you're nervous."

"Yeah I am but you're also sick."

"I'm sick and I don't even feel it; I'm disabled; I'm not incompetent. Get over yourself, for fuck's sake," Michelle said, kind of wanting to just slap her on the ass to get her out of the house. "Go. I'll call Alan. We'll chill. Watch a movie. If I need you I will call you."

"You sure," Faith checked. "That guy..."

"Fuck, woman. Take yes for an answer. I'm sure. Go out with your girl. I swear..."

Chapter 6

They decided to do away with the dinner for this date and just met at Andrea's place. Faith put her phone on a loud ringer for her wife in case she got a call; they sat on either end of the couch.

"You know how to cook?" Andrea asked.

"A few things," Faith answered.

They sat on the couch and looked at each other and giggled.

"So, I...I don't know what to do," Faith confessed.

Andrea paused. Then: "Okay. We'll talk about it."

"That seems weird."

"Honey, that's because you've done only the default for so long. Queer folk like us have to talk this shit through. I mean, if you knew what you wanted I would roll with it but, because you don't know, we should talk."

"That makes sense."

"Okay. You got it. To make sure, an example: would sex with your wife have been better if you talked about what you wanted before you did it?"

Faith thought about the things she did want. The ones she hoped Michelle would somehow psychically connect with. They never happened.

Andrea watched Faith. Faith's eyes closed in slow realization it was precisely as Andrea said.

"Seems simple, right? I mean, I am not surprised even if you did a lot of reading because some girls like us don't like to talk about this stuff in public. "

"Yeah."

"Okay. Well, first thing, we're using condoms. I got an STI screen—"

"Me too," Faith said.

"You did? Great. Great. Still condoms, yeah?"

"Of course."

"Now we might not fuck today, but we might. Just have to have that all out there, ya know?"

Faith nodded.

"Do you care what we call each other's parts?"

"I don't know."

"I like girldick," Andrea said and smiled at the play on words. Faith grinned and nodded.

"That's perfect."

"Mine is kind of lazy but it still works. Yours?"

"Same," Faith said. Andrea heard a catch in the word.

"You don't want though."

Faith shrugged.

They sat there in silence, allowing the awkwardness to sink in. Then Faith spoke before she could stop herself:

"May I kiss you?" Faith asked, surprising herself. Andrea smiled.

"You may."

Faith leaned over and pivoted herself up onto one knee and moved her face closer to Andrea's.

She hadn't kissed another woman—or anyone but her wife for that matter—since years before she met Michelle. As she tried to allow herself to feel what was happening, she noticed more things: the citrus flavor of Andrea's lip gloss, her lips softer than anything she'd ever felt, how she smelled like good quality makeup. Was that a whiff of a laser session? It didn't matter.

Faith kissed Andrea and Andrea kissed Faith.

They parted. Faith slipped back into her spot on the couch.

Faith's phone rang; she had a special ring tone. It was Michelle.

"It's..."

"Yeah. Okay. Answer it."

Faith got up and picked up and swiped the answer icon.

"Hello, dear."

"Fr—" Michelle halted on the start of Faith's deadname. "Faith? I am so so sorry to bother you. I need you to come home. It was Alan. He...just come home. Please. Now."

"I'll be there in 10."

"I'm sorry," Michelle said, but there was something wavering in her voice.

Michelle ended the call and Faith already was heading toward the door.

"I had a weird vibe from that dude," she said, "I'm so sorry. Something happened with her and I don't know."

"Do you need help?"

"No," she said with no hesitation.

"Okay. Would you like help?"

Faith paused a moment, breathing heavily. Her brain not behaving at all. She had always said no. Always always always pushed people away.

This time: "I," a bit more hesitation here, "I don't know."

"Okay. Then I'll come with. If nothing else I will know who to punch next time I see him."

$%^&*()&^%$^%&^*(*)()

They said nothing as Faith drove and Andrea just kind of held on and tried not to grimace as Faith weaved between lanes of traffic on State then turning north on Jefferson then merging into another road, speeding the whole way. The names became as meaningless to Andrea as Faith took roads she didn't know existed in an effort to shave off minutes.

The thing surprising Andrea the most was how Faith was utterly concentrating on the task. She was unsure of Faith, if she had to be honest with herself, just her sheer and constant awkwardness, but it disappeared as she smoothly and deftly broke several dozen laws in a given two-mile stretch of road. Her wheels didn't even squeak as she took wide turns. She was utterly confident and focused and thought of nothing else other than how to get home to her wife.

She almost wanted to say something to Faith but she was afraid of breaking flow.

When they silently turned the corner onto Faith's street, they saw the lights from the ambulance and the cops and wait—no, was that three? six?—cop cars all around. They parked on the side of the road.

"Nice driving," Andrea said.

Faith looked at her to see if she was joking; she wasn't. She didn't get a lot of compliments. "Thank you," she said.

"Let's go."

Faith was out before the words reached her.

%^&(*)(%$&%*^&()

A uniformed cop stopped Faith and Andrea as they approached the house.

"I live here," Faith said. Then: "She's with me," and pointed at Andrea.

"Okay sir," the officer said.

"Ma'am."

"Yes, ma'am. Sorry sir," the officer said. "Is your wife in there?"

"She should be."

"Okay. She's okay. We just need to finish asking her some questions."

This was when the stretcher emerged from the front door. A sheet covering a silent lump.

"Is that Alan?" Faith asked.

"Yes sir."

"I'm not a sir. What happened?"

"We're still figuring that out. Just give us a few minutes for the detective to finish the statement."

"Fine."

"I don't like cops," Faith said to Andrea as she stepped back a few steps.

"Same."

A few seconds of silence and assessment here. It didn't help illuminate the situation what-so-ever.

"What the fuck happened?" Faith asked.

"I don't know but he said Michelle's fine. So, we have that. Just give it a few."

True to the cop's word (surprising them both), a minute later another person approached.

"Mr Newbaure," a man came out wearing a cheap suit and approached the two women.

"It's Mrs."

"I'm sorry, Mrs Newbaure. My fault. Mrs Newbaure, your wife gave us a statement. Do you own a..." he pulls out a notebook and pages through it, "a 'Cold Steel SRK.' Nice knife, by the way." He puts the notebook back.

"Yes. She killed him?"

"Yes, ma'am. We have taken the knife as evidence."

"She's okay?"

"Yes. She's a little shaken up. I don't see a need to bring her in now, but a full investigation is still required."

"Can I see her?"

"Only a moment, ma'am. I need to ask a question."

"Yes."

"What is the nature of your wife's disability?"

"She's paraplegic. She can't move her legs. It's a lower lumbar. I'm sorry how is this relevant?"

"Just confirming statements, Mrs Newbaure. You're free to go in; the officers inside will tell you where they're still working. Please keep us abreast of any travel plans for the next couple months. Likely nothing."

Faith looked at the officer then ran inside. Andrea walked slowly after, trying to absorb what was happening.

If it weren't for the cops everywhere, it would be a nice small home, single story, nothing huge. But there were cops. And they were everywhere.

Andrea stood by the doorway and tried to take it in: Michelle (at least Andrea [correctly] presumed it was Michelle) sat in her wheelchair in the living room, blood all over a plain nightgown. Faith was next to her, one arm wrapped around her as a paramedic stitched up the back of her forearm. A bruise was almost visibly growing on her other arm, which was draped over Faith. No carpets, Andrea noticed. A stream of blood drops from the living room back into where (she guessed [again, correctly]) the bedrooms were. A pair of crutches was leaning against the wall by the door right by her. She noticed they were decorated with duct tape, the kind with patterns. This pattern: Ducks. The television was large and took up a good portion of the wall, and the couches were arranged with a lounger on one side. There were few end-tables and free-standing items. Paths were clear of clutter. The effect was less minimalist aesthetic and more utilitarian. Everything placed everywhere had a purpose. If she leaned over a bit, she would see small hooks in the wall, holding the crutches in place.

"Andrea?"

Andrea didn't hear and kept looking around.

"Andrea?" And this time she heard. Faith was calling her. "Hon, watch out behind you."

A couple technicians (another correct assumption) were behind her.

"Oh. Sorry," she said and stepped aside. They moved with urgency down the hallway. Andrea approached Faith and Michelle.

"Uhh. I don't know why I asked to come. I should be going."

"Oh. I'll drive you," Faith said.

"No. No. You got stuff here. I'll use an app or something. Michelle?"

She looked up, kind of not focusing on Andrea for a moment. Then making contact, "Hello, Andrea I presume. Sorry for the mess," she said and then laughed. "Sorry. It's been a fucked up night."

"I can see that."

"I'm so sorry," Michelle said. "I...I didn't know who else to call.

I'm sorry to stop your date."

"It's fine."

"Yeah. I know. But I'm still apologizing because it seems like the most normal thing I can do right now," Michelle said.

"Well, then apology accepted."

"Faith has been super excited for the time with you. I hope that...yeah."

"No. But it might take a bit. I get it. Faith...you can call me when things calm down a bit?"

"I'd like that. I'm so sorry."

"Don't apologize. I mean really this is super fucked up, as you said."

"Yeah," Michelle said, with her eyes wide.

"Bye."

"Bye."

Andrea walked out of the house and down the street a bit. She wondered what to do. Basically tell someone, right? Talk through this. What the fuck just happened? She just met a murderer? Self-defense? What? She pulled out her phone. She flipped open her contact list and pressed "Marc."

"Hey," he said. "'Sup?"

"I need you to pick me up. You're not going to fucking believe what just happened," she said.

Chapter 7

A week later, Faith was in a waiting room for her wife's (new) therapist. She looked at the text she was going to send to Andrea. How do you address what happened? How weird was it? Do you ignore it? Bringing a date to a murder scene? Who does that?

Faith wrote and rewrote the message.

"Hi." Deleted.

"Hey." Deleted.

"Hi." Deleted.

"Hey. Can you believe that?" Deleted.

"Hi. I know we left each other..." Deleted.

"Should just talk," Deleted.

"Hi." Deleted.

"Okay. That was weird. If you want to meet again." Deleted.

"Hi. That was weird. I'm sorry. If you want to meet again I'd be happy to see you." Deleted.

"Hi. That was weird. I'm sorry. If you want to meet again I'd love that." Deleted.

"Hi. That was weird. I'm sorry. If you want to meet again I'd be happy to see you."

She paused at this one. Sighed. Tapped "send."

$%&^*( )&^%$^

Andrea ate popcorn while her phone buzzed. She ignored it. She was deep into a movie. It was actually a hate watch of a movie. *The Danish Girl.*

She had downloaded it and had a copy just to see not just how awful it was, but how god awful it was. She watched the movie about once a month from a file on her laptop.

Every scene was horrible, building on the last. The movie was about how Lili Elbe became one of the first people to undergo bottom surgery.

Andrea hated it more every time she watched it. At this point it had evolved from direct criticism of the movie and it's nauseatingly over-acted, well into the society and culture that said this story was okay to be told by cis people. The movie was almost over, the point when they wheeled Lili out of surgery at the end and she's dying of something and all that and really Andrea was upset about the genital centric nature of the whole trope.

On a previous viewing, she tried to see it abstractly, as a film, for its cinematography, wardrobe, and so on. But that lasted all of about 15 minutes before she took to her Mastodon account blasting it again.

"Jesus, Andi," was a response. "You watch it every month. Let it go."

But she couldn't. It ruined literally every movie she saw with "that guy" in it. She let it finish. The credits were rolling as she picked up her phone to post something about "Trans life porn" or something, but whatever it was dissipated into a sea of neurons when she saw the message notification from Faith.

She read the two messages.

"Hi. That was weird. I'm sorry. If you want to meet again I'd be happy to see you."

The timestamp said the next message came a minute later.

"If you don't that's okay. No hard feelings. Thanks."

She sat there wondering what to say until the credits ended.

$%^&*()ꙮ

Faith was holding her phone and wondering when (read: if) the response would come. It finally did. Her wife's therapy session was almost over. She looked at the time and judged it to be enough to recover when Michelle came out of the room. She swiped to the notification.

"Yeah. It was fucked up. What your wife did was brave. I wouldn't mind seeing you again if things are calm."

Faith did a happy dance for a second. Then she thought about her wife in there, discussing killing her boyfriend because her wife was out a date with her potential new girlfriend. It seemed wrong to be even jiggling a little in joy, but it didn't matter, did it? Nobody saw it. But then she was hit with guilt as soon as the good vibes started, Faith wondered if it was the right thing to do. Was she allowed to be excited? Was she allowed to be this way? And, of course, to be honest, if she was a good person and a straight cis-het male she would have been home and then her wife wouldn't have had to stab some man of her acquaintance and leaving her to crawl away bloody as he died from a un/lucky strike into his leg, cutting the femoral artery.

I should have been home, she thought. Then she corrected herself and muttered, "He should have been home."

The receptionist looked up, an eyebrow arched, then back down.

Of course, Faith knew that this was completely nonsensical. Because if he had continued to exist then, if she were to be honest, he probably wouldn't have much existed much longer. Suicide has a way of sorting those kinds of things out.

But it was done. It happened. The what ifs, she tried to tell herself, were not important.

And yet they continued in her head. She wondered how she could have done things differently. How she could have been so selfish? Her heart started to beat faster. Faith knew exactly what was coming.

She closed her eyes and started to try to control her breathing. She tried to breathe so her diaphragm expanded, deep and whole and slow. It looked like she was sleeping; okay it was pretty much exactly like she was sleeping. But she was sitting straight up.

"Faith," Michelle said as she opened the door from the back. "Were you sleeping?"

"No. No. I'm fine. Just doing breathing exercises."

Michelle looked at her.

"Yeah. Okay. Sure."

She did the walking thing and Faith watched her and felt bad again. She looked at Michelle. There was a bruise on her face from where he hit her.

She locked her knees somehow and pitched forward, catching herself with the crutches, walking with some odd grace. She did use a chair some days. Though Michelle knew she would someday have to all the time.

She approached Faith. Faith rose, kissed her on the cheek.

"Ready?"

Michelle nodded.

They walked to the elevator. The elevator was old and was mostly decorated with cheap wood paneling and a rattling air/fan unit in the ceiling. It probably was in dire need of service, considering it occasionally squeaked as it went down (but not when it went up earlier).

They said nothing to each other in the elevator.

Walking to the car, Faith stepped ahead at the end and opened the passenger door. Michelle approached and positioned herself and lowered herself into the car. Faith took the crutches and threw them in the back seat. There was a mark near where the foot pad hit where the foot pad had hit a thousand times before. It was a mixture of dirt and grime and water and grass and random detritus too small the sweep up or out of the way. The fabric in the back, stained as it was, hadn't ripped yet. Until that day.

Faith just crooked her lips and then got into the car.

Faith pulled out of the driveway, each neither noticed nor nothing said anything to the other in a good long while.

$%&^*&( )-+

Michelle went to bed early, an effort to just recover still more after all that had happened. After Faith checked the wounds on Michelle's legs (healing) and looked at the cut on her arm (same), Faith tucked her wife in; she ended up in the living room, playing her video game. Again. It had been just over a week since she played and she already noticed the degradation in her skills.

She ventured into the multiplayer player vs player format. Destiny calls it The Crucible. Faith couldn't tell if it was named after the play (she had been taken to a version of it in High School of a local college), but there it was. In her game, however, she chose the "Kill Everyone" gameplay.

The idea of the game was simply to kill as many people as quickly as possible and try to avoid that fate, too. Straightforward. Simple. Yet, complex. After a round she regained her footing, it focused her attention completely while her subconscious worked itself into and out of knots.

If you're looking at someone playing or writing or composing or painting or coding or anything really of the sort and they hit what scientists and nerds call a "flow state," it looks exceptionally boring. It looks as if nothing is happening. Maybe their eyes are even closed. Their fingers flying over a keyboard. Or their hands on a controller so effortlessly making the on-screen representation of themselves jump through the air as if made of feathers. But for the person doing the task, there is nothing quite like it. There is nothing else occurring in their mind but a focus on the next word they are writing, and even then not really because their mind has already moved on to the next sentence, next paragraph, next chapter, and has started constructing things related to them all; or the coder who can keep the whole system in her head as she constructs a module to extend the use case, or a painter who does not look up from the minutest details of the painting to look at the larger scheme because they know it will be utterly perfect. Sometimes, at play, those same engines fire, those same mechanisms hit, and there is nothing but the task, the moment. It wouldn't be a stretch to say this is a path to enlightenment, at least for a moment. Because when Faith loses it and starts over thinking and analyzing and losing interest is when she falters, she loses a sense of almost happiness—or really a sense of not-sadness—but also a second or three of pure in-the-moment-ness that is so easily shattered by anything from the grumbling of a stomach to a cat knocking over a thing too close to a counter edge or the oddly audible buzz of a cell phone, which is what it was this time.

Andrea.

The text message: "I am free next Friday. Wanna see a punk band? I know the drummer."

And, for once, Faith didn't mind her flow interrupted. Not at all.

$%^&(*&$%^&(*)

The Friday of the show, Michelle looked at her wife. She knew Faith was always expecting a negative answer.

"You sure it's okay?"

It had been two weeks since that incident. She didn't feel okay being alone. She really wanted Faith to stay home with her but she knew what would happen would be the same thing that had been happening every night. She'd talk about killing a man.

Last night it went like this, all fast and between sobs and weeping and laughing in a way that was more scary than funny.

"I mean he just came up to me and I told him I wasn't feeling up to it. I was worried about the infection and maybe it would be best if we just hung out. I thought I might blow him but I really wasn't feeling well; my stomach just aching for a reason to empty itself. I didn't want to promise. I wanted it to be comfortable with him. I wanted to just relax and watch a movie. You were out and I was happy for you and I kind of knew what was going to happen and I know you had been looking forward to it so I just wanted to be out of the way you know but he he he just kind of was nice for a while like he was but there was something in his voice, ya know, a kind of 'over it' kind of tone and I could hear it totally and I was worried he was pissed at me but in a way I trusted him because, well, I had to. I asked him if he wanted popcorn and he made some terrible joke about popping my cornhole and that wasn't funny at all. It was just kind of gross. He had made comments before but that was weird. So I didn't make popcorn. He asked me if I wanted to snuggle in the bed and then I said yes so he picked me up and carried me— like you do, but...less gentle—and threw me on the bed. I looked at him after I stopped bouncing and he had this look on his face that was blank, you know, kind of blank. You've seen it. Maybe. But you know how it feels I bet. Just needing something I could give him and helpless there right in front of him and he crawled in bed and told me what he was going to do and I wouldn't stop it. He put a hand on my throat and I...I remember liking that but I never think I can do that again. I don't know but did he take that from me? I don't know but he told me what was going to happen and he was going to roll me over and fuck me and there wasn't anything I could do about it and he told me I was a cripple with a...sorry...sorry...you for a husband he called you that and he just said nobody would believe me if I told them what happened and that I better just take what was coming and he turned me over and I felt along the edge of the bed and the dresser. I remembered the knife oh god I remembered that knife we kept in there for reasons and I remembered how you used to hold it against my skin and I would love it and beg for small cuts and you would make my guts go gooey and that was good but this was bad and I remembered it there, Faith, I remembered it and I slid the drawer open as he opened his fly and pulled down my pants but before he could get them down I grabbed it and turned myself over and plunged it into his stomach and he looked at me like more surprised than scared and I pulled it out and but he pushed me off the bed and I fell on the ground and I almost cut myself on the knife but somehow I didn't and he got out of the bed and walked around and started calling me bitch and cunt and all those names and he came toward me and I sat up and shoved that knife into his leg and pulled it out and the blood showered out like some cartoon or horror movie or something it came out in great pulses as I imagine his heart pumped it out and then he just fell straight down and I crawled away and crawled to the chair and the phone and called you and the cops and I'm so sorry I didn't want to I just wanted to have a quiet night why did he have to do that?"

She cried and Faith held her tight and listened to every word and just took it. Took her wife's unending stream of consciousness. How he punched her and pulled her down the hallway. How he held her and took off what work she could for it and held her tight and loved her and tried to make it right and keep everything good.

Today Michelle wanted to emotionally dump again. To feel her wife's arms around her again but she didn't know if she would ever be right again and, somehow, she just had to realize and accept incompleteness and imperfection and move on purposefully not just trying to float on through life, to be somewhat purposeful.

So, when Michelle looked at Faith's eyes, as she wondered if she would be okay alone tonight, with the blood cleaned up and the house to herself, she knew she might not be but instead Michelle lied and said, "Yes."

Maybe it would be good to play some games. Read a book. Do something else; get a pizza; call her mom. Something!

Or cry all night.

%^*&( )%*^&($(#

After the door was locked and latched, Michelle didn't feel up to walking, really, so she sat in her chair and pushed herself to her room. She climbed in bed and laid there for a while. She tried to turn on the TV, but the batteries in the remote were dead and she didn't care enough. She threw the remote somewhere (it ended up under a pile of dirty clothes), and reached for her tablet. It was still charged, so she scrolled through that.

About 10 minutes into a re-watch of House of Cards, she felt short of breath. She closed her eyes, and tears and huge sobs came out in such a way anyone would guess she was mocking someone else. But she wasn't. She tried to slow herself, to allow herself time to breathe but her crying would not let her. It came wave upon wave and her brain quickly went meta telling herself she didn't really feel that way and it was too much and to stop stop stop as if anyone really gave a damn about her crippled ass. She opened the messenger app for Faith and then stopped herself and then started writing a message and then stopping and starting again.

But not hitting send.

She wept for a while. 10 minutes. 15 minutes. Eventually the strength in her withered. Frank Underwood talked to the camera and her tablet asked if she was still there. She cried more and hit yes. Was it an hour or two or a half? She couldn't rightly tell you. There was nothing she could tell you but a stream of wailing, deep and high and in between.

It was like that for a long time. She didn't do anything. Didn't call her mom. Didn't do anything for a long long time.

It was, really, not much different from any other night, even with Faith here. The same, except Faith gave a patient hand on Michelle's back, rubbing. And that was nice but not enough no not enough of course is it every really enough? All people can do is to hold you and be nearby, they can't fix the shit. They can't fix the feeling of Alan's blood pouring out around the knife as it slid home, deep into his gut. They can't fix the look of surprise and disbelief when he looked down and said, "You killed me, you goddamned bitch." And then what? And then what the fuck can you do if you can't fix it? Just sit there and hold her and rub her back and tell her that you're there. Because of course you're here because you're too devoted to be smart enough to do anything else. This was how she concluded Faith was too good for her. But Faith always told her, because she could say this stuff between the cries and the sobs and the punches on pillows, that Michelle was good enough, that Faith wanted to be here, to be nearby and to hold her and rub her on the back and tell her she was there, that that is what she signed up for those years and years and years ago, whenever it was. And for a second Michelle hated Faith because Faith was too good and then she quickly realized that was stupid stupid stupid and there was nothing she could do that was even considered logical in that moment because she had killed a man. He had come for her. He had targeted her. Had planned this, could see how things were arranged and set up even in the house. That night was hers in her head forever. Memory does not replicate, it re-renders scenes anew, slight changes to fit models of otherwise incoherent thought because reality never makes that much sense. Not at all. Even those key memories, those things you never thought you would forget like the time at the park where you told your dad you were a girl, the time at the ballpark years before when you hit a home run and the ball goes further and further out in the more time passes between the reality and the re-call. Between the reality and rubs on the back and the promises that it'll be better even though the only thing that changes isn't what happened, but it's we've re-written our memories enough to be able to live with what we have done. Oh god oh god was it that in fact? Was it that? Like the time the man tried to rape us and we plunged a knife into him. Until he died. On top of us. And we had to push him off with arms and no balance against legs that only rarely supported the body.

How did it happen? Really?

$^%&^*&(

The band was not in Faith's first choices. She was more pop than punk. Faith thought the bassist was cute. Well, the bassist was cute, short black hair and dark skin. She couldn't help but look at her through that gaze, even for a moment. When Faith met another trans woman it was instinctual, this inventory of appearance. She felt bad about it, but it was a habit she could not break. She wanted her and wanted to be her.

Everyone on stage was trans. Which was amazing, but that was it. She had to admit it was neat to see women like her on stage mak-ing noise and art for the world even if the world couldn't be assed to listen to them. Then, of course, came the comparisons of herself to the other girls. The process was automatic now but it wasn't without emotional effort.

She didn't get the music. The punk thing. It was like a saw blade with an uneven beat. The drum set had a stylized black flag logo on the bass drum; instead of the black bars they were trans flags. Faith appreciated that, at least.

The song ended and faith could barely hear the singer say, "My name is Jessica. This is the—" then noise as the drummer started banging on her drums. Without delay they went into another song which Faith thought sounded like a wall of noise.

But Andrea was in the pit.

Faith watched Andrea fight through a giant crowd of queers, punks, and assorted miscreants. She jumped up and down and shouted the words back to the band. She knew every word.

Someone pushed Andrea from behind very hard. Not a light bump, but a sincere shove and, if she hadn't fallen into the person in front of her, she would have taken a tumble. As it was, the force distributed among the crowd and by three or four people in it had dissipated.

Andrea turned around and saw him. She recognized him. Fucking Nazi. At her friend's show. Usually they came in groups. But this one,this one she knew, was a loner.

"Jordan," she said. She would know that face anywhere.

She had gone on a date with the dude. He claimed to not know she was trans. The conversation was a little like this:

"I just wanted to appreciate how you treated me last time like a woman. A lot of guys who date trans girls don't particularly treat them well."

"Wait, you're a he?"

The date quickly devolved from there.

He claimed to not have read Andrea's profile. What a bunch of bullshit, but maybe true. Regardless, she hadn't seen Jordon in person in, what was it, 10 years? He went a different way in life. She saw the "14" tattooed on the back of one hand. She knew "88" was on the other. He had messaged a photo of them, middle fingers extended, years after their series of two dates, after she changed her number yet again, in a hope to get away from the harassment.

Faith looked on, unsure what was going on and why her date was suddenly still. She followed Andrea's gaze to the man, shaved head hidden under a hoodie, violence in his eyes. Faith knew the look and moved around at an angle, pushing gently between others and kind of just making way.

"You're dead, tranny," he said. And this time Andrea heard it. And if Andrea heard it, so did Faith.

Loud chords from the last song echoed out of the venue; Jessica screamed into the mic, "This is a classic, 'Nazi Punks Fuck Off,'" she screamed and the buzz saw guitar started accompanied a voice that was about a million times better than the original. That's not narrative flourish that's just objective fact.

Andrea positioned her feet for the fight as she had unfortunately done many times before. She hadn't been trained or anything but had her fair share of fighting. Many more were before she transitioned, but some memories are long.

Jordan strode toward her with purpose. Andrea dropped her stance, bent knees. She brought up her fists. The time slowed, like it does. That song—that god-awful song performed beautifully—was only about a minute long, she prepared herself for a fight. She scanned the crowd for any bald heads, any compatriots of Jordan. Was he alone? He could have been.

He came within striking distance and pulled his fist back for a haymaker. Andrea could see it coming and prepared to evade and counter. The song was finishing. Feedback was waning.

Andrea couldn't see if Jordan was surprised or didn't even register when Faith stepped in with a body check that knocked him back on his ass. The fight was over before it could really begin.

Faith yelled at him, "Oh, I'm sorry. Were you going to hit my girl, fucker?"

Jessica and the rest of the band, silent on stage, were watching too. A bunch of the crowd realized what was going on and turned around. They all followed the lead

This was a punk show at some run-down venue. Three out of four toilet stalls in the men's were broken. Only two were labeled as such. Was there security? There might have been. But they were all gone after the ticket taking was over.

"You got any friends? You want more? Or are you gonna get out of here before this tranny dismantles you?" Faith asked; her emphasis on the "man" in dismantles particularly harsh. The small crowd watched, quiet, kind of stunned.

Jordan looked around. He hadn't come with anyone. He had come to just enjoy the music, maybe, but the trans were there. And this band with the whole lot of them. He could have been ignored if he stayed to himself and stuck his tattooed hands in his pockets. But then he saw Andrea, that dude who hadn't told him she was a he. He swore her profile didn't but it did and he's a fucking Nazi, so who are you going to believe?

He got up, "I'm done."

"Good," Faith said and turned away from him to give Andrea a hug.

Jordan watched, turned, and walked away, Faith's turned back more of an insult than he would admit.

Andrea held her tight, still half-surprised. She had fought so many times alone, so many times without help, just spectators, like today, without anyone to be with her. She wondered about Faith and why she would have done that.

"Well, fuck. Holy shit, Andrea," Jessica said from the stage into the mic. "That's your girl?"

Andrea turned toward Jessica, looking up on the stage, Faith with her arm around her. "Yeah. I would say so."

Andrea turned back to Faith. They looked at each other. They closed their eyes and kissed.

They did not hear the applause or the start of the next song.

Part II

"Que ist das, mes amis?"
— Julie Knispel

Chapter 8

Words give way in enthusiastic consent. Words give way to hands and to fingers. Words give way with sounds and gesture replacing them. Words give way to breaths. The breaths both slow and sometimes sharp in the dark. Words give way to a silence made comfortable, then the comfort of pressed lips and finger tips. Words give way to sensation and cessations, to stimulation and penetration. Words give way to lust which is just love made manifest, love made madness, and love made magnificent. Words give way.

Andrea held Faith and Faith held Andrea. They kissed and kissed and groped and fumbled like any two new lovers, newness and excitement and desire all co-mingle, forgiving mistakes made in the moment because it's all so new and neither of them really knows what the other will do and what touch may come and what desire may rise and fall. It comes and goes as they work through this, as if they were the first women to do this, as if they were the first to look at another woman like themselves and give way to glee and happiness and simple joy that they do not have to justify themselves, they do not have to hide themselves, they do not have to explain themselves.

Two women, in a darkened room, sheets dirtying, pillows supporting, love making. Complete and real.

And when it's over, because all things are eventually over, they cry. They both cry because it had been too long since they or the other had been held and touched and loved and felt at peace with another person and smiled at each other and looked at each other without judgment for their bodies. Can you imagine that, for once, for a time, they were okay and not put upon by expectations and demarcations and delineations of roles?

Faith hugged Andrea tight and she wished she could hold tighter, bring her ever closer and hold her within her. Not like that, but just to keep her and to know someone was there in the moment for her and not wanting something or planning something, and not just using her. But wanting her. Just for her. Only her.

Andrea held Faith, feeling the same. Feeling still. Feeling at peace. Her own fingers pressed into Faith's back, leaving small white marks when she repositions them.

It's raining outside. The two women burrow under the blankets to kiss one another, to wrap arms and legs around one another, to let their fingers roam all over one another yet another time in the dark, as the rain comes down steady and constant, distant thunders no concern, the blue covers moving, reflecting light from the television. The television playing whatever came next per algorithm. A cat sitting on a couch, paying no mind.

$%^*(&)&^%$&

Faith woke up to a kiss. Andrea stood over her, a pair of lips on her forehead. "Good Morning, Starshine," Andrea said. "I hope you slept well."

"I did. And you?"

"Like an angel. I'm preparing some breakfast. Omelet okay? I had another toothbrush so I put it on the sink. It's the red one. Mine's green."

"Got it."

Faith sat up and looked out the window, the river was visible just below. Before this morning, she had only been in at night, and never could see the geography of where the apartment was, so she didn't realize they were right on the banks. The loft opened to a view of downtown across the river and north and south of the river as it meandered.

"This is a great view."

"Yeah. It's nice," Andrea said from the kitchen. "Ham and cheese? Simple. American fries?"

"Oh my god, that sounds perfect."

"Great."

Faith walked to the bathroom, then back out to get her phone because she couldn't tell the color of the toothbrushes. They both looked red to her.

"Fuck."

She went to get her phone and check on the app, but as she unlocked the phone she was worried she had missed some vital notification, some message. No pressing notifications came in the night. She went back and checked with her app and chose the proper toothbrush.

Andrea finished the omelets and placed them on the kitchen table as Faith came out of the bathroom.

They looked at each other across the food and ate. Grinning at each other and giggling they finished breakfast quickly and again found themselves on the bed, lips upon lips, hand upon hand, legs interlocked.

All around them and across the water, the rest of the city awoke, unaware of the bliss in a small apartment by the river.

$#$^%*&( )&$^#

Michelle looked out the window as her wife sat in her car, crying. She hadn't even come to the door yet. Just pulled in the driveway. Even from this far away Michelle could see the sobs as her shoulders rose and fell.

She sighed

It was a long night. When she finally stopped crying, she cleaned a few things, but Michelle didn't feel like doing much more than some dishes and some cleaning of makeup brushes and putting away some laundry. Then she went to her office and tried to draw. A portrait she had promised a friend, but when she picked up her pencil for the sketch work nothing came out as she thought. It came out dark and she kept picking up her red pencil and adding.

She knew what she could do. But she wanted to just put it behind her. Her drawing time was meditative. It was when she didn't live her life in the past or the future. A flow state, again. Like her wife, she ached to feel nothing, to be as absorbed in the act to as to disappear into it. She had drawn before, of course, but as she lay in the bed at the hospital after her great fall, she picked it up again. Michelle's mother brought her one of those laptop desks and a pad of drawing paper, a set of pencils.

For a while she drew lots of pictures of trees and leaves and Autumnal landscapes. She thought it was funny, the pun implied there. Ha-ha. Get it. Fall. Hah!

The graphite black pencils gave way to colored pencils; the details grew finer, the inspiration darker. Fall gave way to winter landscapes. She learned how to do her walk. To take care of herself again. The landscapes were still dark. They were obsessed with cold and death for a long while. Then she met Faith.

Faith. In the car. Sobbing.

"Fuck," Michelle said.

She went to the front door, opened it, and headed down the ramp toward Faith's car.

Faith saw her coming and wiped the snot off her nose with her forearm. Michelle grimaced. Fucking Gross, she thought. She can be so gross. And then one of her intrusive thoughts came to mind and she shoved it away.

"What's wrong, honey?" Michelle asked as she approached the car. Faith had the door open, her purse in hand.

"I...I don't know."

"Okay, honey. Let's go in and talk about it, Okay?"

"Okay."

Michelle turned herself around and started back up the driveway. She felt a slight acceleration as Faith took over pushing, just as she always did. "I got it, honey," Michelle told her wife, gently, because sometimes Faith was a little too helpful.

"Okay," Faith said and stopped pushing. Michelle pushed herself up the ramps and into the house. "How was your night?"

"Fine, dear," she lied. "Now, what happened? Why were you crying?"

"I don't really know. I just...I like her. I felt so comfortable with her. I could talk to her about everything."

"That's good, right? Did she do okay with you?"

"It was wonderful."

"So?"

Faith sat down and Michelle came up and stopped in front of her.

"It was," she rubbed her face, further smearing the last vestiges of makeup were already spotty and smudged and more than slightly askew. "It was perfect," she looked at her wife. Pause. "We had sex."

Michelle nodded. That was pretty much as expected. Still weird, she thought, to hear it said so plainly. No fanfare. No apologies. As they had discussed.

"So, what about it?"

They looked at each other for a minute.

"I really don't know. I'm all mixed up. I liked it. I feel guilty. I love how she touches me." A beat. "This is weird to talk to you about."

"Weird to listen to. But tell me."

"I just felt right in her arms. Like...like how I used to feel with you."

$%&^*()

Andrea waited until Faith left, then gave her ten minutes and she called Vannah. "Faith stayed the night."

"Tell me about it."

"Sure, but I have to tell you about the concert."

"What happened?"

"She fucking took out Jordan!"

"Jordan? The Nazi puke you went on, like, three or four dates with?"

"No, no you fuck. It was two and he never read my goddamned profile," Andrea said. Vannah chuckled. "I can't believe he still has a hard-on about it years later."

"Anyway, so what did she do?"

"She just...stepped into him and he fell down."

"What?"

"I don't know. He was coming at me, I could see him coming at me with his hand in a fist and then she was just there and was a wall. He ran into her and bounced off and went skidding across the ground. An immovable object."

"Wow."

"Yeah."

"She was a total badass, telling him she would dismantle him and shit. Then, as he was getting up, she turned her back on him."

"Uh oh."

"No no. He...just fucking left."

Vannah laughed, Andrea could hear her breathe in and hold a cigarette. "Scared the piss out of that Nazi motherfucker."

"I can neither confirm nor deny a puddle."

"Oh, girl, I have to meet this woman."

"Yeah. You do."

"Make it happen, then. So...then what?"

"Oh, then we fucked."

Vannah waited for the silence to get uncomfortable, then, "That's all you're gonna tell me?"

Andrea laughed. "Twice."

Chapter 9

Faith was alone, a small cutting board in front of her and a half-empty glass of orange juice. Most people stopped this kind of shit in high school. She didn't, though not as often now. It had been a year or two. The last time was a bad batch though, nothing more than a shimmer on the outside of buildings. The things were mushrooms, what they called the "Magic" variety, though they were really just chemicals. They tasted terrible. Hence the OJ. But they helped sometimes to clarify things to her.

She thought about Michelle. Did she regret what she said to her? No. It was true. That was a day or two ago. Or what her and Andrea did? No. Andrea texted regularly, but some work deadline was approaching for her and she had to concentrate there. Faith...not so much. And her video game was no longer holding her interest.

Michelle was at work. The antibiotics from the infection of the sore on her leg had taken their course and it appeared normal and healing at the checkup yesterday. The cuts and bruises from....him...same.

Faith called in to her job. They wouldn't miss her. She was some interchangeable middle management lackey.

She was a goddess on the floor of that punk show. Taking down that guy. Then adored in Andrea's arms, and then she came home to Michelle. No, Michelle wasn't bad. But it was something different, something mundane, about the come down. It felt further than before. It was like leaping and falling when wings do not sprout. Alternately made of hope, made of fear, Faith knows her despair like an eagle knows how to ride thermals. She also knows sometimes winds will die out and she will be left tumbling through the sky, if she could even climb and try to fly. Not long ago it was different. Not long ago. She had it. That feeling. Of presence. Of love. Of acceptance. But it mapped onto a presentation that was not right. That was when she was not able to live her truth, as the kids say. She had to live a lie, as other people would say. She would just say it sucks and it was how it was.

Before, it happened like this: She would dress and make herself up; occasionally she saw a girl in the mirror. This was the moment she lived for for years. Those few moments before she scratched her nose and noticed the hairy backs of her hands. The few minutes before she noted her stubble stuck just a half mil out of the makeup she had caked on. That moment, right there. That acceptance. That feeling of "okay."

Push it away, don't look at it no more, the brows are too broad and the shoulders to match and the hands too big and her feet stuffed in too small shoes that fit fine long-ways but across the top crushed down her arch. But as long as she was home, it was okay. There was no need to walk too much.

"I gotta lay down," she said, and she did. She laid on the couch and faced the back and smelled the farts of decades that had passed with the gas and the thought made her smile a little at how the gas molecules were, like, embedded in the foam of the seat cushion and just kind of held on there until she put her face down and the different weights let long trapped gases out and all over. She looked at the threads of the couch and the pattern-less cloth developed patterns: smiles and faces and legs and arms and breasts and cocks, but mostly the face thing because that's what happens in brains. Faces. Faces.

She stared and stared some more and eventually dozed.

Her dreams were vivid, but unremembered.

When she woke a short time later she found her shirt damp with sweat. She had to pee so she walked to the bathroom. The walk was not difficult, and there was just a slight wobbliness of reality. One of the undulations of psychedelics she was aware of, being this was not her first rodeo, trip, space out, time, place, event, feeling, happening, or whatever the fuck this was.

She got in the bathroom and took down her pants as she stood in front of the toilet. She looked down and her cock had disappeared, somehow. She couldn't find it. She shrugged. She sat down and peed.

She left, went to her room, and laid down and sweated and the rest of her trip was a chase after patterns and colors, and in the early morning before the dawn with the moonshine still visible outside she woke up and felt, for the first time in a long time, happy. Not a fleeting lifting, not a momentary lapse of despair, but the cessation of the self-loathing and an escalation of mood above the baseline. This was the goal, actually. The trip was the toll paid for this feeling. This relaxing, almost normal feeling.

Michelle slept next to her, her face cute and adorable. Faith looked at her for a minute and saw the start of the wrinkles on her face. The slight lines across and her smile lines and her face utterly relaxed and her chest rising and falling. But that feeling in her mind; that feeling of complete adoration and love and she felt as if she could die right then looking at her wife; she loved her utterly as much as any human had ever loved another human as she watched her wife sleep.

Which is creepy she had to admit. But right then she was glad that Michelle was there sharing the bed with Faith. Even if they rarely touched, rarely kissed, and no longer made love. She felt a connection to her, as if Faith's atoms were wrapped about Michelle's. This was cheesy as a fucking grilled cheese sandwich made with "bread" that was actually burnt cheese, but the mushrooms were still doing their thing at least a little. She thought about how the photons had come out of the sun and bounced off the moon which illuminated the bedroom just slightly and bounced all around and off her wife's face and then right up into her eyes, their journey of a trillion miles or whatever it was ending right here, no more existing.

She was still pretty high, now that she thought about it.

She went to the bathroom again.

There are people who would say Faith's trip was not real, was not reality. But was what they experienced either? Maybe, man, the world is a simulation and we're just waiting for the kid to turn off his new universe simulator and then poof we'll be just the mote in some god-child's eye. Or maybe this is all a solipsistic nightmare and there really is only one conscious mind in the entire universe and it is yours and everything disappears and re-appears when it affects you.

Dear reader, the fuck do we know?

$%&^*((*&^#%$^&%$*^%&^()

As soon as Andrea got home from her time with Vannah and felt okay with what had happened—no, fuck that, she felt good! There was a whole hour where she felt hopeful and not like death was poking her on the shoulder, pointing to his watch and making that stupid rolling hand "hurry up" motion. Just an hour. Then she got a message on her phone.

Sitting in front of her computer, she unlocked her phone to look at it again. She found the message from her mom's phone number. They never talked. Only occasionally she would get a message. Short. Status updates. This was one of those: "Grandpa Earl's dead," it said.

That was an hour ago.

She had a work deadline, but instead of doing anything, she sat and stared through her computer monitor. Her mouse occasionally flicking to the other screen, refreshing a Reddit thread that she couldn't even remember opening, her Twitter scrolling by insistently like a river of words, her Facebook notifications rising and falling, her instant messenger windows blinking, her whole mental world was praying for silence but she just shoved in more noise: music and a slowly changing slideshow and even the TV on for just more noise and she didn't do anything.

The windows were open for her to work. To code. Whatever it was she was doing this week. Something with a web site. She put a line down. Stopped. Deleted it. Made a few lines. Tested what she had done. It was fine. Pushed the file back up to the server. Pulled another. Push, pull, edit, sometimes just adding some white space and a comment block—not even real comments just the empty space for them—or declaring some variable that she thought she might want to use but never got around to.

She spent hours at this. Occasionally, tears would come.

Earl. He wasn't a grandpa. What was he? He was, like, this guy in the town she grew up in. He was this big guy, and he was big in the emotional sense too. He took in all the queer kids that got kicked out of their homes and he helped get them back on track. Gave them a bedroom with a lock on the door and he was there with food and a kind voice.

Parents sent the cops after him all the time. Claimed he was fucking them. Nah. Was just this jovial fat dude who was a gay Santa, kind of. Sent out cards all over the country to kids he had helped, he got so many in return they would cover his dining room table and fall onto the floor whenever his cat jumped on there.

Andrea went to see him, once, when she was little. When she was just learning what she was. See, Grandpa Earl wasn't too familiar with girls like her, but he told her to come back in a couple days and he would have some information printed out, a couple books and the like.

And he did. For fuck's sake, he did. Not just the popular ones but good ones and a couple email addresses of places not too far that if Andrea did get to a computer she could totally send them a message and ask for more information.

She didn't ever do that, but she remembered reading through that pile of papers late into the night and crying, and giving Earl a hug before she ran home.

Was information that hard to come by? Yes. That was a long time ago. Before the Internet was everywhere. Now she had it all there. Twenty years ago, she didn't even really know what a computer was. She had even less idea of what she was, if she had to really admit it to herself. It was all just vague hints and gestures and hope.

Was she a girl? Earl wasn't too helpful. He said that she would know and whatever it was that she decided it was okay. Of course, she didn't look too much like a girl, with the zits and patchy facial hair and greasy hair on her head and all. But that was normal, really, for someone of that hormonal makeup.

But she remembered his face as he just listened to her talk about how she had once tried on a dress and she just twirled around in it and now he was dead. Dead. And nobody else would be able to go to him.

How many queer kids had he helped. Thousands?

She wept for the quiet hero; one she hadn't thought of in years, but who came back to her larger than life, his laughter and smile carrying her through that evening, showing her the path to this very day.

But she still wept. She cried because grief is a weird thing. Grief for people you never met. People you never knew.

She was like this for two days.

Periodically she thought about calling Vannah. She didn't want to bother the woman. Something. Something in her head told her no because she was taking care of her mother or something today, right? Or work? She didn't even know just ticked off a dozen shitty reasons and rounded up to a good reason. What about Jessica? She was in a van, doing her thing. So Andrea was alone. She sat in silence. She cried.

Faith never came to her. It was too soon to reach out for this. To burden her Faith with it. Though of course that was silly. She realized it as she dismissed it. She fucking was there when Faith's wife had just murdered a dude. Faith had knocked the fuck out of that Nazi punk.

But brains do what brains do, after all.

%$&^*(()^&%

Jordan yawned. He was hunched over, staring into his computer screen. There were a cluster of dead pixels on the LCD and he had to scroll down to make sure the line said 8 or 0 and, well, it doesn't really matter what it was. He was scrolling through the forums of his favorite forum, one for Nazis, confederate sympathizers who were open about the hate that informed their heritage.

He had just gotten home and wondered what happened. He thought about posting it but didn't because, well, they would make fun of him for getting his ass handed to him by one of those...ya know.

So he scrolled idly, trying to think of how he felt precisely.

He looked at the weed he had. Decided it wasn't what he wanted. Took the whisky and poured a little of it into a cup. Then he followed it with some cola.

The depths and hidden undulations of hate are not probed by many people, so they only hear noise where there is melody. But the melody exists for all humans who hate. There are hidden songs of hate and they are great crescendos that build and build for years, growing louder measure by measure, the beats slow and unforgiving and deep. And when you look under the noise of the world's orchestra, within the wailing woodwinds and gnashing of teeth against strings and the pummels of the drums, the melody of a thing pokes through. That simple beautiful thing amidst all the god-damned noise becomes all you can hear. It becomes the key that the static fills. It becomes silent against the noise during the rests. It guides you through the chaos and discord and havoc and you still feel how you feel but you're still overwhelmed but it's this melody you can focus on: the object of your hate.

That was who Jordan was thinking about. A nice little melody with the occasional counterpoint of the woman (he stopped, "corrected" it to "man") who knocked Jordan down, sent him sprawling in front of all those people.

Who was there was kind of unimportant. The fact he went to see an all trans band was not even in the realm of a dissonant chord.

His ears and heart focused on the melody of his hate: Andrea. Faith provided counterpoint.

Chapter 10

Four days later, Michelle sat across from Andrea for the first time at a dining room table. A glass of wine was at either's hand. Faith was in the other room, assembling dinner.

They were quiet.

For a while.

A long while.

"This is weird," Andrea offered.

"Oh, thank god," Michelle said.

They laughed.

"Yeah," Andrea said. "I've not done this before. But Faith is cool. I really respect her."

Michelle smiled, did not let her face read what she really felt about how that was phrased. Respect. That was a vague kind of word. One can respect another for any number of reasons.

"She's got quite a head on her shoulders," Michelle said. "And, not that it's interesting to me, but apparently quite a nice behind, too."

Faith overheard this as she walked in with the entree and side dishes stacked expertly in her arms.

"What is that supposed to mean, dear?"

"Oh, I'm just telling Andrea you have a nice ass."

Faith looked at Michelle. "Are you gonna make this weird?"

"It already is weird," she said. Andrea grunted in agreement.

"Okay. Yeah. It is." Faith put the dishes out and sat herself at the table. They all looked at the food slightly askance.

Andrea, "Though this looks delicious. What is it?"

"A dry curry. I usually don't cook vegan but this is a vegan dish I learned how to make. It's quite spicy."

"That's great."

"Tofu, green beans, onions, peppers, other peppers, and a curry paste. Not terribly difficult. A bed of rice; I am into regular white rice but some people prefer the jasmine."

"It's good," Michelle said. "She cooks the tofu enough so it's not just a mushy paste."

"Cool."

They dug in. Ate for a while. Words of no consequence were exchanged. The typical fare of daily itineraries and annoyances at workplaces and commutes. After a short while, that was exhausted, even with three people present. They were avoiding the obvious topic at hand. They knew it; all of them. It was not so much dancing around the topic but wearing a radioactive suit and keeping a 50-mile radius from it. The small talk was not giving them anything other than a way to fill the air with words.

"Can I propose something?" Michelle asked.

Andrea said, "Yes," before Faith could step in. Faith knew what was coming. She didn't know how she knew, but she could almost guess the next words that were going to come out of her wife's mouth, verbatim. Many years had made Faith's mental model of Michelle mostly accurate. She wouldn't have been far off the exact wording either.

"Radical honesty for the rest of the evening," Michelle said. She unlocked the wheels and moved her chair closer to the table, locking them again. "I have no strong feelings about what you two do sexually so that should be easy. But I do love Faith, and so I worry about her."

"All around," Andrea clarified.

"I'm not agreeing to it," Faith said.

"Well 2 out of 3 curry eaters agree."

Andrea and Michelle both looked at Faith and nodded.

"Do whatever. I can always keep my mouth shut."

"Of course, dear," Michelle said in that withering way that pretty much ensured Faith would participate.

"You may go first, as a guest, Andrea."

"Oh, thank you. How did you get paralyzed?"

Was Faith or Andrea expecting this? Hard to say. But Michelle had had that question often enough it was kind of expected but she figured she would at least try to teach her a little lesson on dealing with disabled people.

"First, uhh, that's not appropriate," Michelle said.

"Okay. So, what were you going to ask me?"

Michelle looked at her. "Fair point." A sigh. "An accident. I was nineteen. A nice day. Climbed a tree. I fell. Almost killed me. Didn't immediately cut things off there. I tried to get up and movement exacerbated the injury. "

A pause.

"Sorry," Andrea offered.

"Yeah."

Another pause. So much silence in a good discussion.

"Andrea," Michelle said, "I love my wife. How does that make you feel?"

Faith stiffened a little.

"That's great," Andrea said. Her tone was upbeat, and Michelle probed the nuances of her face and her resonance and her intonation and word choice and found them acceptable. Sometimes the training and years she had sat in a chair in front of a patient was useful.

"How come?"

"Because I do not want to be hated by either of you. That you love her and know what's going on is a great start. I mean, I don't know what I want in this. I know she seems nice and if you two are on the up and up that makes it easier for me."

"Jealousy?"

"Nah. I mean, I imagine there might be a circumstance where I would want to do something, but she can't. I mean, a month ago," Andrea said and waved her hand and everyone, including the recently replaced carpets, understood what she meant. "But things happen. Things occur. Life is life."

"That's very well thought out and clear," Michelle said.

"Thank you. Now me?" Andrea said.

"Sure," Michelle said, "Unless that was your question."

A chuckle.

"Why open the marriage? You're straight, that's all?"

"That's a big part of it. Part of it is I don't...I don't know. I wouldn't say I'm asexual because I certainly do feel sexual attraction a lot. Maybe just I'm particular?"

"How so?"

"I like men. And I like manly men. And I like that...smell. She doesn't smell right anymore."

"I'm sorry," Faith said.

Michelle looked at her with a mixture of pity and love and disgust. "I still love you. Just not that way."

A pause.

"You know, Faith," Michelle said. "Remember when we went to the keys in Florida? Remember how we didn't fuck because of my period? But we just held hands and cared for one another every day. And we were just happy there for a while."

"Yeah. "

"I feel that way now. We both could be better for one another, yes. Of course. But I am happy to see you come home every day. I am happy to sit on the couch with you and know you are there. I am happy to have you in my life and I can't for a minute imagine what it would be like any other way. I am so happy you are able to be yourself now, even if I wasn't always the best at that. I am happy now with us. "

Faith looked at her wife and fell in love again and again.

There was silence for a minute.

Michelle said, "I gotta ask. She's my wife. I want to protect her, in that small way I can. So, why?"

"Why what?" Andrea asked.

"Why are you interested in Faith?"

"Because she seems like the kind of person I would like to know. She's cute and fun and can hold her own in a fight and all the rest."

"A fight?"

"She didn't tell you?"

"No," Michelle said. She looked at her wife. "Faith, did you get in a fight?"

"I ended one," Faith said, which surprised both her and Michelle. She wouldn't have spoken like that terribly long ago.

"How?"

"Some asshole was going to punch Andrea, so I stopped in the way and knocked him down."

"That's it?"

"Was enough. He ran off after. Didn't see any friends."

"That seems rather fortunate."

"Yeah."

"So, what happens when you see him again?"

"Why do you think I will?"

Michelle shrugged. "Paranoid feelings."

Faith got up and sat next to her wife. "I get it. I promise it's done. He won't hurt you, okay?"

Michelle looked at her wife. Though Faith still had awkward and sloppy eyeliner and eyeshadow, her eyes themselves showed something different, something hard and firm and real. New? Maybe. Maybe. Certainly not a common thing. And Michelle believed her.

^&*(*&(^*(*%^^*$%&*

Andrea closed the door to her car and breathed in deep enough to make herself yawn. Twice.

Was it weird? She had to confess it was. But some of Faith's behaviors were pretty obviously tracked to her marriage to Michelle. Though Michelle was capable, Faith made it a bad habit to rush to take care of her, which often annoyed Michelle and wore out Faith. It was weird to see from the outside; because usually folks are so involved with how they interact with people regardless of their axis of oppression (to borrow a SJW [for want of yet another phrase]

phrase). So, to see two persons interact as they did, given their long history and deep grooves of habit, was, at least intellectually, interesting.

Emotionally, who the fuck knew. The meeting was more for Michelle and Faith than Andrea. Andrea knew she liked Faith. She talked to Marc last week and told him she kind of really liked Faith for who knows what kind of reason. Sometimes a protector for a trans girl who always protected herself. When does the crust people coat themselves with against the world become an exoskeleton that prohibits movement? Other poor metaphors applied.

Also, that day, Marc told her he would be moving to a coast for a job opportunity. She cried over this. Another person gone. Vannah had moved home near Chicago to be with her mother and that wasn't too far, but a thousand miles away was something else. Something too much to even plan a day around.

She, really, only had a couple local professional contacts left. And Faith. That's it.

That isolation, though. It's not a good spot to be in, she knew. But there wasn't a trans group here; and her attempts to make one a few years before was met mostly with teenage trans guys and crossdressers. Nothing wrong with them, but they were not what she needed. She didn't want to help drive some kids to the clinic in Chicago on their 18th birthday to get their T shot—at least not for the 10th time—only to have them disappear a month later when they decide they don't need a girl around anymore. Or at least an older one who wouldn't let them fuck her.

Was she a little bitter? Sure.

The crossdressers were fine, but just different. At least until they decided to transition themselves, but they rarely did. A lot of flirting between them, and with the idea; a lot of excuse making; a lot of lamentations about loss of jobs, wives, and children. Also, but unsaid: the privilege of being seen as a man. Which is quite different from being one, she knew. That kind of idea would get her kicked out of many on-line support groups. But she had it. Even if sometimes it seemed a little off. She was willing to be wrong, but hadn't seen how that was happening.

Fuck.

The place before, she got fired for coming out, after all. Well, not for it, of course. But something else. Not long thereafter. It was obvious what the real reason was. Nobody invited her to meetings any more. Nobody asked for her input. She'd been tasked with taking minutes in meetings, but they never took minutes before. Cliché writing on cliché wall.

There had been the survivor's guilt about the layoffs the year before, but to know something was coming like that, just completely unaware of when it would hit. She was almost happy to be called into her grand-boss' office. Coincidentally, that company no longer existed.

Now her job was remote. Fine. Slack chats and emails. But she could realistically spend days without physically speaking to someone; all interactions moderated via screen. Which, again, fine. Just it was sometimes not.

But alone.

They all left, didn't they? They left or disowned or fired or just no longer were with her, corporeally. This wasn't up the road, a day trip as she said. Just so many fucking miles. Over and over her mind went over how to see him, and she had no idea why. She was just alone here.

She could move, too, she thought. Maybe closer to Chicago. Maybe. That queer scene, at least from what she saw, was a little weird and cliquish. Like they all were, she figured.

One time she went to Burning Man in 2015 and she went to a trans camp. Everyone was polite. Nobody was rude. But it was clear they didn't care if she died so long as she was out of their camp. They didn't say anything, but it was just an insular group.

She had more luck just wandering around her camp. Introducing herself, being awkward. She met a friend she still talked to, but she lived in NYC, so why bother really? Fuck.

The more she thought about it the more she wanted to just kind of crawl into Faith's arms but that wasn't really an answer, was it? That's how those couples who only stay home and watch TV are.

They don't go out they don't do anything but be with each other because they are scared and don't want to be rejected. Fuck. Fuck. She got home, walked up the stairs, and sat at her computer.

The clock on the wall said 5 o'clock. Technically she was done working, but of course she wasn't. That wasn't in the cards at a startup. But regardless of her technically being done but not really being done working she was emotionally done working. There was always more to do. More pixels to push. More code to generate.

She just wanted to eat on her own somewhere. Around other people but not with other people. Just so she would get some of the feeling of socialization and none of the risk.

What was Faith doing? Andrea wondered. Then she tried to push that out of her mind, because the goal wasn't to become co-dependent. The goal tonight was to get out and maybe do something. Would she? Would she?

She shut down her computer after making nothing and picked up her iPad. She swept away the notifications, stared at her home screen for a minute, then two more. She put the tablet down. Then picked up her phone and repeated the ritual.

She stood up, grabbed her phone and keys and wallet and shoved them in various pockets, then out the door. She had no idea where she was going.

^$&^%*()&&^%&(*)

Faith answered the phone in a daze. It was near 1 AM. The ID said "Andrea." But the voice wasn't hers.

"Hi. This is Kyle at The Office. Your friend Andy—sorry, fuck—Andrea is here. I got her keys, but you're gonna have to come get her. She's too drunk to drive."

"What?"

"Your friend is drunk. She can't stay here. She asked me to call you. So, I did. Now are you gonna get her or what?"

"Yeah, yeah. Gimme 10 minutes."

"Fine," before he hung up Faith could swear she heard the t-slur. But she could have been mistaken.

She wasn't.

^%$&*(&^^^%$&^*((

She arrived after 9 minutes. The bartender said "10 minutes, huh?" as she walked in. Faith gave a stare the Nazi at the punk show would recognize; the barkeep kept back then.

"Andrea?"

"Faith. What are you doing here?"

"The bartender called me like you told him to."

"Oh. Oh okay."

"C'mon. We'll get out of here. Take you home."

"I don't want to go home."

"You can't stay here."

"Home is alone," Andrea said; Faith took a second and parsed it.

"We'll go to my house."

"No. Your wife."

"Michelle is fine. She's sleeping. We have a couch. Can you stand up?"

"She doesn't like me."

"She likes you fine. Get up."

Andrea tried, succeeded. Barely. "Why you nice?"

"Because I am and I like you."

"You like me?"

"Yes," Faith said without really thinking, her hands-on Andrea's shoulders.

"I like you," Andrea reiterated.

"Good. Can you walk?"

Andrea belched. Faith caught a whiff of it and it had the faint odor of vomit which caused her own stomach to turn just a bit.

"Did you puke?"

"Yeah."

"Where?"

Andrea gestured toward the back, the restrooms.

"Okay. You're with me," Faith said, tucked an arm around and under Andrea's arms. She looked at the bartender, who watched the whole scene still unsure what to make of it. "She good with you? We'll get the car tomorrow."

The bartender tilted his head like a confused puppy. Then he said, "Yeah, all good."

Faith nodded and lead her friend and lover to her car and gently into it. Buckled her safely in place and closed the door. She walked around the car, looked both ways, got in, took her home.

%$^&()*(&^

The drive-time discussion:

"Why were you drinking?"

"Leaving."

"Huh?"

"My friend Marc is leaving," she said, slightly less slurred, still slowly.

"Marc?"

"Yeah. My only friend around here. Gone."

"I'm sorry," Faith said, swallowing the difficult feeling of not being included in that group.

"Fucking gone, man. Everyone fucking goes."

"I am still here."

Andrea turned her face toward Faith and smiled; her drunkenness exaggerating it all.

"Good! Good!" she half-yelled. "But—"

She stopped for a few seconds.

"But everyone goes. My parents. My sister. My friends. Everyone. They go everywhere and I'm fucking stuck here. Here. ya know? What the fuck kind of place is this city?"

"Why are you stuck here?" Faith said.

Andrea laughed. "That's why I like you. Cut through the bullshit. There's no reason, really. Com—" a gross belch," Ugh, gross. Comfort? Maybe? I don't fucking know."

"I see."

"Yeah, yeah okay. I...I don't hate it here. It's comfortable. It's close enough to stuff but far enough away to bitch about being far away and I don't know. But it wouldn't matter where if I went everyone is elsewhere. Vannah's in Chicago and Marc will be in fucking Oregon. I don't want to move where I can't even pump gas. Julie is in Jersey. Annie is in the old Jersey—the island between France and England and shit—which is kind of neat but I got fucking nothing there. Eva moved to Turkey. Kate in Maine. Nobody. Nobody here. Even Cass moved to fucking South Carolina! Not a soul but you and Michelle and I'm already fucking up ain't I?"

"You're fine," she said. She meant it.

$^%*&(^%%^*&()

We've seen this scene before, dear reader. We've seen Andrea sleeping on the couch, we've seen Faith lay a blanket upon Andrea. We've seen her doze off, cared for by Faith.

Faith went to her room and laid next to Michelle, who was up on her phone, scrolling through something unimportant.

"She's here?"

"Yeah."

"Drunk?"

"Passed out."

"She on her side?"

Faith sighed and could not remember.

"I forgot."

"She could choke on her vomit, dear."

"I know. Okay. I forgot."

"I know, dear."

She sat up on the side of her bed. Michelle propped herself up on an elbow.

"You okay?"

"Tired." Faith said. Her tone betraying a wariness deeper than the word itself.

"You should go to sleep," Michelle said. "I got her."

"You sure?"

"Yeah. I can't sleep anyway."

"Holding the bright light 5 inches from your face doesn't help."

"No. But go to sleep. You did good. I'll watch her. Just get my chair."

Michelle swung one leg then the other onto the floor as Faith rolled the chair to her side of the bed. Michelle lifted herself off the bed and fell into it. Faith knew enough to not help unless called upon. At least this time. Sometimes she forgot.

"Sleep well," Michelle said. "Kiss me goodnight."

Faith looked at her.

"Do I gotta ask twice?"

Faith almost fell coming to her wife and sat on the bed and kissed her on the lips.

"Sleep well, dear. You did good for her. Okay? You gotta work tomorrow?"

"No, it's a holiday."

"The third? Weird. Okay. Well. I'm just not scheduled until the fifth. I think they're fucking with my schedule again. Cutting my hours."

"Assholes."

"Yeah."

"Why are we talking? Go to bed."

"Thank you."

"For?"

"Kissing me. Taking care of her. Kissing me, though."

"Dear, I still love you," Michelle said. "I really do. Now I'm gonna make sure your girlfriend doesn't die. Okay?"

"Okay."

And Faith's sleep was dreamless.

Chapter 11

Andrea woke to the snoring of Michelle, who slept in what looked to be slightly uncomfortably (though was not) on the oversized recliner. Her chair was nearby. A little bit of drool on her chin completed the look.

The sun was out and its warmth was pulling the dew from the grass and bushes outside.

Andrea rubbed her face and looked at her hand, bits of mascara and eyeshadow and glitter were on her hand. "Shit," she whispered. What did she fucking do? She talked to Marc and he told her he was moving but that was just the latest of the things. But that was part of it. The latest of the things. The drinking.

"Fuck."

Checked her phone. Fancy alarm system had rung her a dozen times this morning, all dismissed.

"Fuck."

She logged into her home camera system. She had one because of course she had one. Because what does a paranoid woman do with her time and her earnings. Honestly, she often thought about taking the whole security system down. Nothing appeared out of place. And nobody outside the door. She turned it off.

After going to the bathroom, she chanced to rinse out her mouth with the mouthwash they had, without a toothbrush that seemed it might be the best way to go. It hurt after a few seconds but she persisted, eventually spitting it back into the sink.

She closed her eyes and turned her face toward the mirror, ready to open her eyes and be once again her mother's son. When she finally opened her eyes in a dare enough to shatter herself, a woman looked back at her, makeup askew, hair tattered and stringy from sweat. She sighed and shut off the lights.

In the living room Michelle was still asleep, a few small noises from the bedroom and Andrea walked toward it.

The house was not terribly big, in fact she walked through it within minutes, all one floor.

Faith was in her bed on her phone.

"Good morning," Faith said to her.

"Good morning."

"How are you today?"

"Confused. How did I get here?"

"You drank too much. The bartender called me and I came to get you."

"Where was I?"

"The Office."

"Oh."

"Presume you walked there. I made sure your car would be fine if you hadn't, but I got your keys."

"Oh."

"Come here."

Andrea came to Faith and laid down next to her. The alarm clock radio said 8:34 AM. The plastic had been cracked on the speaker once from an over-aggressive attack on the snooze button. But Andrea didn't know that. And the scar had mostly faded from Faith's hand. She wanted to remember the time for some reason.

"Headache?"

Andrea shook her head.

"Don't get hungover usually."

"Impressive."

"Practice."

"How are you feeling today though?"

"Okay. Better. It meant a lot that you came for me."

"Of course."

"And Michelle out there?"

"She watched you until she passed out because she can't sleep lately. With that thing," she said. She looked at the spot of paint that was on the ceiling that wasn't there before they had to repaint because of the blood.

"Yeah."

They held each other for a while in silence. A bird outside sang, like they do. The neighbor's lawnmower started, like they do. The air conditioner kicked on.

Andrea turned in Faith's arms toward her. They kissed once eyes open. Second time eyes closed. Third time hearts open.

=\\:"_=%^&*()

Michelle never dreamed of herself. That's not true. Occasionally she did. But not tonight. And for the record she still was paralyzed in them when they did happen.

This one was a movie. Dreaming in narrative. Does that mean something? She didn't know.

She dreamed in fits. Vignettes

A rain on a cloudy day. A bank robbery. A night at a discotheque. Is that a thing? She thought it was. She imagined men dancing and in a break of her fourth wall, them interested in her and she didn't feel scared.

Another bank robbery. Fireworks. They ran through her head like movies.

What does that mean? She wondered sometimes if it meant anything.

It didn't. Unless of course if she thought it did.

:==/*€$\#\;#__]µ´{´µθµ¿

It was a kind of after sex discussion that sometimes happens. The arm in arm and leg over leg and emotions open somehow.

Faith asked about a scar on Andrea's leg.

"That was.... before." Andrea said.

Faith nodded. "May I touch it?"

Andrea waved the invitation. Faith touched the shiny skin, a half dozen inches long.

"I never felt real. I tried to be real but it was all puppetry. It was all a ruse. I never felt as if this body were real. Until a few weeks on estrogen. Then I finally felt...like I came into focus. No. I'm mixing metaphors. I don't know. The puppet. There is something there. I don't know. Just the disconnection. I used to tell Marc...because I've known him so long," she stopped here. Breathed heavy. Started again. "I told him I always felt a weird delay in my emotions. Ran through a filter. And my puppetry was only a clumsy re-creation. I don't know. I still don't have words. Just...gestures toward reality

"Can an emptiness be a pain? The total accumulated gross—pun intended—feeling of muted emotions." A breath. A moment. A hand brushed through Faith's hair. "Is that old life real if you never felt it?" Faith shook her head. She didn't know. "It's okay. I just wonder if transition is what actually made me into a real person." Another breath. Another moment. Then she continued.

"That scar. I wondered if I was real. For a while. I was sure I wasn't. I was sure I needed to see. To know. Like...under this husk was I real? That scar convinced me. At least intellectually. I was lucky as hell it didn't get infected. Lucky, I didn't hit anything vital."

Faith bent at her waist and kissed the scar. "I feel lucky, too."

"I only did it once," Andrea said. "It was enough."

"I still do," Faith said. "A lot."

"I know. It's okay."

"Is it?" Faith asked, looking up at Andrea, as if meaning and validation could be found in her girlfriend's (Oh, was she that? [Yes, she was.]) face. But for a moment, the smile from Andrea was close enough.

=\\:"_=,._::¡^´¬·

Michelle woke to the smell of bacon and eggs and coffee and the sound of girlish giggling from the kitchen. She pulled her chair closer, climbed on, and went into the kitchen, where Andrea and Faith were both cooking.

"Good morning, Honey," Faith said.

"Good morning, metamour," Andrea said, then stopped. "Is that okay? Sorry. Michelle."

Michelle thought for a second and shrugged. "It's okay. I kind of like it."

Andrea smiled. "Thank you for keeping an eye on me last night."

"Of course. Don't want another dead body in the house."

This shut everyone up. "Oh, come on," Michelle said. "No fucking humor."

The awkwardness passed after a bit. The ladies continued to cook. Michelle went to the table and started reading news on her phone.

"How many eggs?" one of them asked Michelle. It doesn't matter who.

"Three is fine."

"How?"

"Over hard."

A few minutes later bacon, OJ, wheat toast, and three over hard eggs appeared, brought to the kitchen table by Faith, along with a peck of a kiss on the forehead.

"I could get used to this," Michelle said and everyone laughed. The other two sat down with their eggs and bacon and toast and they ate breakfast together. Because nothing of consequence happened then, that, of course, meant far more than what would be suggested.

Chapter 12

Faith dropped Andrea off later that day.

She talked to Marc via a series of texts. Somehow both having Faith and Michelle about and making sure Marc was not terribly far away via text made her feel better, at least she was not incommunicado with the important people.

She flipped on the computer, logged in to the book of faces and saw a message from Vannah. Her mom had passed. More important than a bio mother. A mother of chosen family. This morning. She saw the time. About 9 AM. While she was in bed with Faith.

A coincidence. Also, a coincidence: The phone ringing, Vannah on the line.

"Oh honey," Andrea said.

"It was time. Not unexpected." It was why she was there. "It's okay. Can you come to the service?"

"When?"

"Saturday."

"I will be there."

"You gonna bring Faith?"

"Nah. I mean, do you want me to?"

"Nah."

"Okay."

"It's not her, ya know. It's just...private."

"I understand."

"I know she wasn't my real mom," Vannah said. "But she took me in. What would I have done?"

"She was your real mom. She was there when you needed, not just when you were somebody you weren't."

"True."

"Fucking crazy woman, though," Andrea said, making Vannah laugh.

"Had to be. You know."

"I know. Live through that shit."

That shit was an unsaid thing. Julia transitioned in the 70s with black-market birth control pills and a back-alley castration. The guy that did it focused mostly on people who wanted them gone for other reasons, but Julia found him and paid him and thanked him profusely when she could finally stand again. The medically established gatekeepers kept her transition away from her because she was too mannish, didn't want to date men, and wouldn't lie and say she would. She also didn't want to move and start another life somewhere. So, she did it her way.

She was a caretaker for a while, an angel among the dying for that generation of men who had AIDS and the stigma that surrounded them. Julia stayed with them at the end. She guessed she had seen 80, 90 men to those ends and a handful of women, some like her and some not. Sarcomas and pneumonias and overdoses people couldn't be sure if were on purpose. She had never done that, if a narrator can be believed; but she did leave people alone sometimes, their medicine unguarded. Sometimes they did what they begged for; most often not.

That was when she took Vannah in. Her birth mother kicked Vannah's tranny ass out when she was 12, catching her in a bra and panties. Then the streets. Somehow, she found Julia before even 2 nights out there. Julia took her in, clothed her, raised her, took her to school. Shared the spirolactone and tried to ward off Vannah's "male" puberty, but failed.

But she took care of Vannah. School. College. The spelling bee where she and Andrea met, though that was before Andrea transitioned herself.

Pay things forward. Pay them back. Take care of mother, of her family of choice. Help her. Hold her. Bury her. Mourn her. Remember her. It's what we do, fam.

#%&(*)_*&^%$#^&*(,

Faith cringed as she looked at the caller ID on her phone. It was her mother, Tara.

"Hello!" her mom yelled into the phone. Her mother always yelled. It was her primary defining behavior. She had recently lost a great deal of her hearing and hadn't yet learned to modulate the volume of her voice. It was annoying, but it was annoying she had also started to, well...

"Hi mom. How are you?" Faith asked.

"Okay. How is my beautiful daughter?"

"I'm fine, thank you," Faith sighed. She waited until she transitioned to start the compliments re: her appearance, but also agreed with dad when she was younger she had a certain dopey druggy slow and fat way about her.

So maybe not abusive or neglectful but maybe the word should be ambivalent? Faith pondered it for a moment as her mother started talking about people who Faith had never heard of and had no interest in and her mother talked as if these were intimates but Faith (rightly) suspected these folks were not as familiar to her mom as she implied.

It was the same every time.

"So, what are you up to?" her mother asked and Faith knew this was more of a prompt to give her mother a topic to ramble on about more than an actual inquiry.

"Well, I had a date."

"A date?"

"Yeah. Michelle and I are testing out polyamory."

"I had a date once your father took me on in the 70s. We met at the arcade, did I tell you that?" Tara asked.

"Yes, numerous times. The whole story."

"Yeah, he met me on a bench on the far side of the mini golf," Tara started and honestly Faith knew the rest of the story but it was like any of the other stories anyone might be aware of. A girl sitting on a bench waiting for her date gets stood up and then the man she marries ends up finding her after he fed about 10 dollars into a pinball machine and Joust.

Whatever. She was still talking, but had edged into how her sister [not a blood relation but a woman Tara had just met and for some reason had just started calling her a sister though there wasn't really a reason to, it's not as if there was a shared experience or a long friendship or deep friendship just Tara was desperate to have a connection of any sort that she just kind of latched onto people.

At least that was Faith's guess.

"So, what is going on with you?"

"I'm just sitting at home right now talking to you."

"Great. I was talking with my girl friend, Meg," her mother continued. In this phrase Faith understood the girlfriend to be not a girlfriend but a girl-space-friend, just a friend that happened to be a girl. The specification of the gender of her friend seemed annoying and unnecessary to Faith.

"Whatever happened to Chris?" mom asked.

"Excuse me?"

"Your friend Chris?"

"Mom, you asked about him 2 days ago. I haven't talked to him in at least 10 years."

"I know, I just wonder what happened. Remember how his mom said you were a bad influence?"

"Yes, I do."

"That was funny. She called up and told me that you were giving him drugs and alcohol and keeping him out all night."

"Yeah, he was giving me them," Faith joined in the recollection for a minute.

"I know. I mean, she was just calling me up and badmouthing you all the time."

"Yeah," Faith said.

"She told me you were fucking him."

This was a new bit of information. That was the thing. Occasionally there would be new bits. The last new bit was her father was stealing pills from Faith's grandparents. Paternal. His mom and dad both dying of cancer had to share their pills with their addict son. This came out a year ago. Facts came out in small bursts, trial balloons, as if she were a political rhetorician.

But this was new.

"Wait, what?"

"Oh, she said you were a faggot and you were fucking him."

"Uhh."

"I know," Faith's mom said. "How redic," she said. She actually said 'redic' as if she were a teenager from the early 2010s and trying hard to fit in but still didn't. "She said she found a condom but you know that could have been from anything that boy did. At least he was safe."

The thing was it wasn't technically incorrect, but it was incorrect in that it presumed several things. Faith's consent being one.

"You know I always knew you were," Tara said, then faded off. As if she didn't want to say what she already actually just did. But she did.

One of those completely coherent moments with her mother, right there. Forcing Faith into her hellish introspective nightmare while her mother went off on a tangent about the interactions of parents when Faith was younger and of course occasionally dead naming her while Faith was not paying attention, but rather than vocalizing at the appropriate moments and then thinking back to one night where Chris had actually put something in the pot he shared with her and fucked her in the ass while she was really too high and/or fucked up on whatever chemical he had sprinkled in the bowl that in retrospect Chris hadn't bothered to smoke out of that night, but his own, so you know this was all on purpose and thought out and part of his plan. But Faith wasn't Faith then, at least not to Chris. Faith was just a doughy ball of boy with a habit of shaving the hair off himself because he had no idea why he hated himself so much after puberty but that wasn't the point yet was it, or wasn't it? She didn't know and retrospection didn't really help. But she did remember insisting on a condom after she consented, or at least gestured at consent with a shaking hand and closing eyes and she guessed he accepted that request, given that, well, poop comes out of there. So when she woke up sore and confused and she knew exactly what women meant about it all. Or at least close enough to be on that bell curve, Faith supposed. Was that kind of the worst part of when she was a kid like her? Did he groom her, knowing what he was doing was wrong and she wouldn't dare report him?

Faith's mother droned on; she moved on to how she had some purses she didn't want any more and did Faith want them because they were so so cute. No. No. No no no.

Faith sometimes wondered if she was not really trans because she had been raped. If it was a cause and if she was just gonna get over it then it would be over and she wouldn't be a she and she would be a he and be happy and maybe she wouldn't have to deal with all the bullshit she had to deal with for the past years. Just get over it. Get over rape. I mean.

"I'm gonna let you go," her mom said.

"Okay, mom."

"Okay. Love you."

"Love you, too."

$%^(&#$^(&)*(_^&#

Jordan. Jordan thought about the dude that knocked him down at the show. That freak tranny was with that other freak tranny, [DEADNAME]. It had been a week and Jordan still felt sick when he thought about how he had just had the air and everything knocked out of him.

"Fuck you, [DEADNAME]," he said about Andrea. "I'll fucking send the cops after your ass."

For what? He was a Nazi. This wasn't some Godwin's Law shit but he was an actual Nazi.

Didn't matter. Not really. He fucking got embarrassed at that show. The fact he was going to physically assault someone didn't enter his mental model of the event. Because that would require too much interpersonal awareness and Jordan was, well, lacking in that. What he was lacking in interpersonal awareness was supplemented by a high susceptibility to confirmation bias.

So, when he wanted to fuck Andrea and she was on the third date (second; he remembered three because he overinflated the importance of chatting over coffee) and she told him she was trans, because, well, it was on her profile. He was not happy. He felt betrayed and lead on by this person and in fact it was his fault quite clearly since it was, like, the second line on her goddamned bio. The only reason he didn't beat her then was they were still in public.

Which is, of course, why she addressed the topic in public. Why there was Marc in the next booth over. Why there was mace in her purse. All planned. This wasn't the first dude that hadn't read her profile. She kind of figured he hadn't but the whole thing kind of confirmed it.

But he felt betrayed, man, as if this was some episode of some practical joke TV show. It wasn't. It was just a date. Blah blah blah. Hadn't even kissed her yet. Blah. Nobody wants to sympathize with a Nazi. Most of all, dear reader, you. And really there's not much to sympathize with. All that can be said in his defense is he hadn't gotten his hand tattoos even at that time. If they had gotten naked then she might have seen the symbols; but he still had those covered by clothes.

You don't want to know about how he was raised in it. How his father beat him once for hanging out with a Mexican kid and bringing home tamales. More than once. More like one time after the other. How his mother was even more vicious because sometimes these things are exactly how you think they are.

Though Jordan still liked tamales. Shit was delicious.

You say you don't want to know how he was taught hate, but you really do know how his overt and complete racism came to be. By society at large, by labels like gangsters and thugs and all the rest. Don't kid yourself. Do not act as if racism is taught only by the worst humans in the world (and Nazis are some of the worst), but it is baked into the society. This society. America. Land of the free because of the brave and the enslaved. Baked into life like corn syrup is baked into a middle American diet. Something ubiquitous and understandable from an evolutionary standpoint but abhorrent.

Because nothing is necessarily in a vacuum.

Jordan looked at himself. He looked at the burner flip phone.

He would do it in the morning. He would call the cops. Tell them [DEADNAME] had guns and drugs and give them the address and hope they fucking shot her, because she was a fucking tranny and should be removed from this goddamned country. That was it. Yes.

He hated that he ever wanted her.

Jordan might not be able to take her out. But the cops could. And they would. Trigger happy assholes. He knew. Some of them were his friends.

He would do it when he was eating tamales at that little Mexican restaurant on the other side of town.

Chapter 13

Outside the funeral home, Andrea parked her car and looked around; Vannah wasn't here yet. She left the engine running for the air conditioner and she just sat there for a moment, eyes closed, thinking, getting ready to deal with people. And lots of them maybe?

There would be people she knew. Vannah, of course. But support group people from the city, friends, family, and chosen family of Julia's. Queers by the dozens, if not more. Political allies and even some respectful rivals would be there. There was even an anti-gay protester Julia had befriended for some reason.

She wondered, again, if all she knew were queer people. Faith's wife? But not quite. Marc was gone. Really that was it. All her friends were queer which was fine and all but just, she thought, a little weird. A little insular. But safer, for sure. Not having to deal with the regular dismissals and arguments about basic humanity.

A mobile safe space, of sorts. If some right-wing reactionaries hadn't rotted out the phrase from the inside.

Off with the engine, almost instantly the humidity outside invaded. Andrea sat a moment more and opened the door.

Once inside, a gently smiling young woman greeted her. Her hair black and straight and down like Wednesday Addams, which Andrea supposed, was kind of the goal. That was fine. This was fine.

There was only one funeral, so Wednesday walked her to the door and with a silent open palmed gesture invited her into the room where Julia laid. Andrea didn't see the name on the plaque, affixed with white letters on a black velvet background.

Was Julia layed? Lied? Laid? Andrea didn't know which one to use and she guessed it didn't much matter. It was laid, for those keeping score. Wait? Was it?

There were not many people there, as it was still early in the afternoon mourning. Vannah wasn't even there, yet, but an older woman and man were beside the casket, looking down.

Andrea circled around the chairs and toward the front of the room and looked over the pictures. Most of the pictures of Julia as a boy. Many more as a boy edging toward manhood, pictures dated until the 80s and then nothing more. Andrea paused, realizing, slowly, what had happened.

She walked to the casket and looked inside, past the two people who hadn't moved.

There was a man in a suit laying in state. He had the face of Julia and the arms and the missing finger on the right hand not even Vannah got an answer for. Her careful eyebrows still in place. A rosary wrapped around both the hands. Hair cut short.

She looked at the people in front of the casket and realized they were looking back at her with faces that could only be properly registered as ugly. Not ugly in the aesthetic sense but ugly as in all they contained, all the emotions and rage and disgust and fear and utter horror one of *them* was in the building mourning the same loss as them.

"Get away from our dad," the woman said.

Dad...suit. That was Julia. One of Vannah's pictures. The scar over her left eye from something.

Andrea remembered a scene from Stone Butch Blues. She remembered Leelah Alcorn. She remembered Feral Pines, Em B, Brandi Chill, Jennifer Gable, Christopher Lee, Kenneth Bostick, Keyshia Blige, Jasmine Collins, Tamara Dominguez, and dozens of others and how they were all misremembered and their own lives ignored by family; that fake connection connecting blood as if it meant anything; that fake and only tenuous connection that thrust them into lives where they were hated and despised.

"Even in death, the cis take this from us," Vannah said from behind Andrea. She wore all black, but she needn't. Her whole being embodied mourning.

"Get out," the man said. "Go. I will call the cops."

"Let's go, hon," Vannah said to Andrea. "There's a reason these wastes of sperm hadn't called her in decades. She sent you cards every year, you know that."

"Go," he said, then he muttered the t-word. Vannah stopped.

"I was going to, but now I am not. You must wait. I am not finished. You are mourning a half a person there. A figment of memory doesn't exist. For why? Her money? She was so much more. Her love and caring and motherhood—"

He cut her off. "Don't call him that."

"Her. That's Julia. My mother. She was more to me than you can imagine, but I know what you did to her. The only reason I don't say it is her soul is still here, clothed in that shitty suit."

"I'm calling the cops," the woman said and pulled out her phone, trying to make a show of it.

Vannah said. "We'll go. Just...may I have a minute," she asked, her voice cracked.

"No," the woman said and the man held her back a second.

"Thirty seconds," he said, as if his balls had grown 3 sizes that day thanks to his single gracious acceptance of someone else's humanity, standing up to the child mourning her mother; he had ignored Julia's calls and letters for years, the hopes for reconciliation, the rest. But her. Maybe she was right, this person. "Then we call the cops," he said. His heart not in it. The fight here. It was not worth it.

Vannah approached Julia's body, the sartorial choices ignored, her face still had the same feminine look it had for so many years. Motherly. Vannah reached out and touched Julia's head and leaned over to kiss her forehead. Only Andrea saw her dangle and drop a chain with the trans symbol next to her body.

They left and went to Vannah's apartment and Andrea held her and let her cry for a long long long time about her mother, about how Julia had taken her in, the whole story again, though Andrea had heard it. But Vannah might come back out to Rockford because there wasn't anything here for her besides her job, though her job was important and well-paying and all the rest. The talk of mourning, of grief, of loss and all the rest. Stories recounted and retold and embellished and more holding and crying until they both fell asleep in her bed, just listening and being friends. Like friends do.

In the morning, Andrea told Vannah about Grandpa Earl. How he had been there for her. That he had also just died.

"He was kind of like Julia," she said.

"There are always people like that. Just sometimes they are too hard to find."

"Those older folk are going and leaving us and we're gonna have to take their place."

Vannah nodded over her coffee, and then smiled. "Well, isn't it good that is that I have been. This girl named Andrea, ya know?"

Andrea rolled her eyes. The point taken.

%^*&()_&^%&(&)#&)#

Evenings happened. Dinners happened and breakfasts happened. Faith went to her job, Andrea went to hers, Michelle went to hers.

This was how it went. Occasionally one would stay at the other's. They stayed mostly at Faith's to be near Michelle in case she was uncomfortable being alone because sometimes that still happened.

$^%*&()_&^%^^*#@%^^#%*

"I'm not feeling your place. Can I stay in?" Andrea said one night a week later or so.

"Do you want me to be there?"

"We're not fucking. That service…"

"No no no. Just…hang out. I'll crash there. It's fine."

Andrea thought for a moment but it wasn't too long of a moment until she said, "Sure."

After Faith parked, she walked up to Andrea's loft. She didn't see Jordan watching Andrea's house from the bar up the street. She didn't see him leave and, even if they had, she wouldn't know where he was going. But he did. He knew the road to the greasy dive of a restaurant.

He had been there every night for a week.

%%&%*^(&*( )&^%*$&^&*(

Once upstairs and firmly snuggling on the couch, neither of them knew the SWAT team was dispatched, prompted by claims of bombs and guns and drugs and the like. Neither of them knew the cops were running up the stairs and were winding up a battering ram at the fragile door until the exact moment of impact. What they did know was someone had busted into the room they were sitting in, holding each other and binge watching some long-canceled television show. The cops yelled something that, if one had super hearing, could maybe be understood as "Police, everybody freeze." The cops ripped the women off the couch and threw on the floor and even Faith didn't know she was making a funny move until one of the cops shot her, a single time, through the back and into the floor, with the bullet eventually ending up on the floor of the unit below.

Before the echo even faded, the shooter started unconsciously constructing a narrative that placed him firmly in the right. As soon as the (rather sparse, being a loft and all) residence was cleared and they all stood around trying to not acknowledge the noise ringing in their ears was not the echoes of a handgun going off in the space but the screaming of Andrea as Faith's blood leaked out. In some, however small, gesture, the ambulance was called quickly. Frantic, the men (for they were all men) in blue. There was nothing here that could justify the shooting that they could find. Not even pot. Just two trannies watching Netflix and one was dying on the floor.

The shooter was a friend of Jordan, this was true, but he wasn't in on the plan. This was, well, an accident, if one believed in such things.

The cops brought dogs and did drug sweeps. The cops handcuffed Faith to the stretcher. When the paramedics left, they had a slow shake of their heads that told Andrea the slowly fading Faith might not make it.

Part III

"You are not artistically pure for turning away from queer suffering."

— Brandon Taylor

Chapter 14

Not long after the emergency surgery, Michelle and Andrea got updates from the doctor, a tired looking woman covered in blood, "All
in all, he is very lucky."

"She."

The doctor stopped, blinked. "Yes. She. Sorry. We removed her
right kidney and sewed up the damage. Because of the close range
there was some burning on the entry wound, but because of being
against the hard floor, apparently, the bullet passed through rather
cleanly. Just hit the organ, a few pieces of small intestine needed to
be removed, too, from the damage. Hence...lots of blood. I mean, it
won't be a fun time, but it could be so, so much worse."

She was wheeled up to the ICU not much later, both Andrea and
Faith stayed near.

As they waited in her room, Andrea held Faith's left hand;
Michelle held Faith's right hand. Into the right was the saline and
pain medication.

She was knocked out from sedation, not from the injury. There
was no coma, just sleep, and her sleep was mostly dreamless. Mostly.
She had two.

The first was a vast salt plain, beset on all sides by mountains and
dust storms. She stood in the middle of the land, aware of the sen-
tience underfoot of a billion mono-cellular organisms working as
one. The smell of iron came to her, rolling into her nose with har-
monies occasionally occluding themselves to noise until the odor
faded to familiarity. There were no clouds overhead. Sweat under

her breasts. The light was as if it were high noon, but no sun was overhead.

She started to walk, in the dream, in any direction because all dreams were meaningless here, except as one subscribes meaning to them. If one waited but a moment a mountain would be consumed by dust and another far-away peak would appear, none of them tall enough to have snow.

As she walked she looked down at the alkaline dust and the cracks that covered the whole playa. Occasionally, garbage appeared and disappeared, absorbed into the dust. A banana peel. A feather. A firecracker. A camera. Did the world have anyone else in it? Were there any other people? She looked around and saw no-one. She stopped and stood in place for a moment, head down, weeping. Her tears sucked into the playa with no hesitation, leaving only the smallest trace they ever existed, then disappearing.

Appearing from nothingness with no warning and no flash, just appearing from nothingness, two pillars of light shooting up were on either side of her, her hands reaching out (were her hands just at her face? No matter, now they were in the light.) and embedded in the pillars, because that's how it was.

She stood there with her hands in the pillars for hours, days, years and the dust around her occasionally pushed in but kept its distance from the pillars and then she realized this was a dream, things like this do not really happen, and so and as suddenly as the pillars appeared, the dream ended.

The second dream was meaningless.

!@#$%^&*()_+_+~

"Why did it happen?"

"SWATted," Andrea said to Michelle. "The cops admitted as much."

"Fucking assholes. Who would do that?"

"I don't know. I think I do, but...who the fuck knows, really."

"What are the cops gonna do?"

"I figured they might tell you, you being her wife and all."

"No."

"Fucking cops."

"Yeah," Faith said, startling Andrea and Michelle both into sitting bolt upright. "What? I am just relaxing."

Andrea jumps to her feet to hug her and Michelle pushes herself up to lean on her legs.

"Oh god," one of them says. Doesn't matter who.

"I'm so glad you're both here. I love you."

"I love you too," they both say simultaneously, the stereo effect overwhelming Faith for a second. Looking from one to the other and tears already coming up.

"Must be the morphine," Faith said. They laughed for a second and Faith winced. Michelle got back into her chair and Andrea stepped back a step.

"So what's my damage?"

Michelle said, "The doctor said they had to take out your kidney and you lost a bit of blood, but you're stable and you should be moving out of the ICU when you wake up, so...yay."

"Good."

"I presume you're okay," Faith said to Andrea.

"Yes. Just scared the fucking ever living fucking shit out of me."

"Same here. Felt different this time."

"This time?" Andrea asked.

"Oh. Army. Shot in Iraq. You didn't...see the scar?"

"I mean, we all have scars. I didn't know you were in the Army." Faith shrugged.

"That's usually a thing for people."

Faith looked at Andrea directly and steadily. "Maybe another time. Please understand. Please drop it."

Andrea nodded. "Sorry."

"It's fine. Just complicated."

"Faith?" Michelle asked.

"Hi."

"Hi. Do you want anything now? Food or pain meds or are you thirsty?"

Faith nodded, realizing what Michelle was doing. A subtle redirecting and attempt to calm. "Thank you, dear," to Andrea, "I am sorry. I just don't like to talk about it, and I just kind of got shot. I promise you I will explain it."

Andrea was slightly perplexed by the exchange she just saw. "It's...it's fine."

Faith breathed in, held it for a second, and let it go out her mouth. To her wife, "I would like some food or water. The pain is okay."

"Andrea?" Michelle asked. "Can you be a dear and go to the nurse's station and tell them?"

"Yeah. Yeah. For sure. No problem."

Andrea left.

"I am glad you are okay, dear."

"Yes. You had me so worried. I love you, Faith. I really do."

"I'm sorry."

"It's okay. It's okay," Michelle said, letting go a little. "I just couldn't imagine you going. You've been here for me and I know it and I really am sorry about the sex thing," she went on.

As if that was all. As if.

"Honey. Babe. Dear. It's okay. You didn't do this."

"If I had just—"

"Stop. Stop it. It's okay. You didn't do anything. It was some freak thing. Some random occurrence and I'll be out of here, presuming the DA doesn't say I was resisting or anything."

Michelle was silent for a second. Her brain offered a quick image of herself jumping out of the window. It was ridiculous. Of course. Legs and all.

"He said that, didn't he? They're going to charge me."

Michelle nodded.

"Fuck."

They sat in silence for a minute. Andrea came back in. A few minutes later a nurse and a doctor came back. A few minutes later, a cop wandered back from the shitter and sat on a chair on the other side of the hall, happy to be getting paid to poop.

The cop looked at the tranny across the hall. Talking to everyone. He knew the charge was bullshit. He knew about SWATting. He knew about it all. It was obvious what happened. But sometimes this shit just went bad and sometimes shit happened like it did. He was glad the tranny didn't die. What was the officer's name? Kizing? Kinzinger. Yeah. That dude would be devastated on that shit. He was already freaking out because everyone knew the shoot was bad and there was no legitimate way to even suggest it was okay. The charges were a bluff; he knew. That other girl, she had some weird video setup in her house. Already off-site, there was no way to not prevent it from getting out. It was a small miracle it hadn't been picked up by a major media outlet.

He knew that couldn't last, though. This cop had even seen some posts on Facebook about it.

Well there was a way. There was always a way for them. But Kinzinger seemed reluctant. Like he didn't want to go along with the plan they hatched right away, those clever SWAT dudes. Ya know.

Shot a tranny in the back. A veteran, though, they found out. Fuck, man. The fuck kind of shit goes through your head when you shoot a veteran in the back, like Kinzinger did there?

Too much shit to think about. Poor bastard.

The cop pulled out his cell phone and texted his super that "she's up."

Way too much shit to think about. Not worth it. Just sit here. Play a game. Troll on twitter. Wait.

Chapter 15

Kinzinger lay in bed and thought about what he had done. She hadn't moved. She hadn't done anything, really. She was just scared and tense and wondering what the fuck was going on.

If they had found something, anything, that would have been something. But also the girl had cameras around her house. Paranoid, she said she was. Apparently with reason. Andrea was her name. The camera feed had already been uploaded and what kind of woman keeps a dead switch on remote control to broadcast her internal stuff to the Internet? Apparently Andrea did. Stored overseas.

So, there was video. He took out the phone and watched it again and again and again.

Fuck. Fuck. Fuck. Paranoia. Justified, apparently.

After she stopped screaming that other one—the paranoid one—yelled they were all on camera and they better get the ambulance there as soon as fucking possible.

Kinzinger remembered the look on her face. Tranny but her rage was...reminded him of his grandmother when she caught him stealing. Kind of this mixture of utter despair, fury, and long-suffering disappointment. Which was just un-fun and totally called for if he thought about it for more than half a second.

Which he did.

Then she turned out to be a vet. The one he shot. The fuck? Not like you can just go and claim this woman wasn't like, perfect. A little Mary Sue-ish but just with this other girl and doing whatever it is they were doing...and married elsewhere?

That ain't illegal. At least now. Or he'd be in trouble, he thought, as he turned to face his wife, who slept peacefully beside him.

Is there really anything worse?

I mean, maybe being shot.

Okay, if she died.

She was on the ground; he was on top of her; she moved her hand or did James bump it? There were a few people, like six guys on two.

Should have done surveillance. No time. 911 call. Some cell phone from some place across town and they were dispatched.

Did he get trained for this?

Got her down; she moved; he already had a gun in her back; did he mean to fire?

Of course he did.

He wanted to kill her. She was a terrorist or drug dealer or bad guy and that's what they knew going in and they all just ran in and yelled and screamed and there were these two people on the couch watching...something...on Netflix but where was the weed, where were the guns and bombs?

There weren't any and he knew this was all confusing but his brain kept jumping and then he heard the shot and felt her tense up under him and start to shake and then stop and what the fuck was that about? What was that? Who does that? Is that what happens?

And you can't hear anything after that, just how loud and the muzzle blast burned his other hand because it was a handgun wait was it a handgun yes it was. He had a handgun out, the rifle hanging by its strap because it was too big for the job. The handcuffs still on his belt.

The handgun. Now at the office; some examiner inspecting it for something? What? It was all there on video that he shot that person. Shot that fucking girl in the back and she didn't do anything? She had served her country or something and then what? Why? Was it because of who she was?

Was that who he was? Adam Kinzinger shot a veteran in the back because she was trans? Is that the kind of man he was? The kind of cop?

Apparently, he was. Apparently, that's exactly the kind of man he was.

He got up and went to the bathroom and looked at himself in the mirror. The clock on the wall (mounted on a faux toilet lid) let him know it was four AM. He usually was up at five. He hadn't slept yet. He was to come in and talk to the union rep. Talk to the sergeant. Or someone. He walked back into the bedroom and noticed the red LED notification light was blinking at him. Usually it was Facebook or something. But this time he picked it up.

"Awesome job shooting that tranny. He fucknig deserved. to die. Maybe next time. -j"

J? Who was J?

What the fuck?

Josh? Joe F? Joe G? Jim? Joe M (a lot of Joes, for some reason)? Jane? Jos? Jose? Jorge? Joshua?

Who would say such stupidity?

Wait. That guy. He had a special hard on against trans women for some reason. What was his name? Jordan? Yeah. That's it. How did he know? They were friends on the Facebook thing, but that was it. Was it? A couple groups about conservativeness and 2nd amendment shit.

Oh. Wait. That other site. So there's that. Isn't there? Some "heritage" one. Fucking heritage of slavers and racism and other such wonderful wonders of the wondrous world never cease to make one wonder why the fuck one would not hang one's head in shame, even if there were other kind-of-nice things about heritage. No? Fuck. At least sweet tea is tasty. Maybe some food.

Pardon, dear reader. That was a narrator interjection.

But the cop didn't think all that much. He just responded, "I didn't want to shoot her."

A second later. "Sure dude. I know you gotta say that. It's cool."

The fuck?

And that was when he got another text. Unknown number.
"Why?"
And another?
"Aim better next time."
Another.
"Did you lose your balls, too? Should have killed it. Double tap."
Another.
"Good job, officer. Doing the LORD's work."
He put the phone down and it buzzed against the table again and again and he picked it up and tried to turn it off but every time he tried to the notification window would come up and return him to the home screen until he just ripped the back off and took the battery out and threw it all on the ground.

The burn on his hand was itchy.

He went back to the bathroom and splashed water onto his face. Then he stepped in the shower and stood under the hot water for a long long long time, until his skin pruned up and the water heater drained and he was left in the cold water, head against the wall. Nothing left in his heart or head but the unshakable feeling he had done so so so much wrong.

(*&^^^%#@#%$^&~!@#!@#

Andrea came home to an eviction notice. Specifically cited was the police action on her property two nights ago as a hazard to other tenants. She had five days. Now four.

"*Fuck!*" she screamed, her voice dropping back into how it sounded so long ago.

She closed the door (new), slid down the inside of it, and cried.

%$%&*^(&)*)(*&^%

The hospital room was cold and Faith shivered under 3 blankets. A slight infection had set in. Nothing serious. It had responded to regular treatments but it still made her run a fever and chills and so...blankets.

The catheter still ran red urine.

Michelle was sleeping on a recliner. Her legs up and a slight snore coming from her face. Faith smiled at the thought. Andrea had to leave a little earlier, get back home. It was fine. It really was. If Michelle was asleep Faith could maybe sleep too but if they were all here then dozing would be more difficult.

They had moved her to a room. It was a double room but there was nobody else in there right then, so some of Michelle's things were strewn about. She thought about sleeping on the other bed, but despite the nurse's claims it would be fine she didn't want to take up room if someone needed that bed. Faith flipped through the TV stations, 30 of them displaying nothing of interest. Old news about political thoughts that was all pointless anyway. Analysis by the ignorant illiterati. Not like the corruption was going anywhere. It just wore a red shirt instead of a blue one this time and hated people like her and she changed the channel again and again and found it all wanting. It hurt her heart, but: click, off.

Faith turned her head to look out the window. This was one of the tallest buildings in the surrounding area. Given she was on the 4th floor that wasn't saying much, but there she was, looking down across the city which, from this height and angle, looked more like a forest with an occasional dot of homes and churches and decaying old factories poking themselves up from wherever the ground was below. However far it was below. Whatever it was. Maybe it was an architecture of the clouds, with trees so high.

In a weird way, she liked it.

Faith yawned.

Like, it never had felt like home. But then again nothing ever did. What does home feel like anyway? Was she safe? Obviously fucking not, if the people with "Protect and Serve" airbrushed on their cars were doing that whole "attempted murder thing." Something about it, though. What is home?

She could move. And in a way, she did want to. But in a way, she wanted to not...to be stubborn and stick through this stupid thing. Maybe that was home, really, where you were stubborn and lazy enough, roots just kind of grew in; they weren't necessarily planted.

That made sense to her.

Just fucking glad she didn't have kids right then. "Oh god," she said to nobody in particular. Kids.

Faith yawned again.

Why? Why no kids?

Just never wanted. Also, the home thing. Also, the estrogen thing and the not having sex with Michelle thing.

Speaking of, they took her off her HRT meds because of course they did. That was what doctors did. "Break an arm? Go off HRT." Fuck. She did as she was told because only they would know because of all the goddamned blood they were taking out.

Both her back and her front were sore. She tried to squeeze the button for more morphine, but she was maxed out for the day, hour, whatever.

Why?

Why?

All she knew is someone had called in a fake tip and the SWAT team came in a shot her in the fucking back and that sucked. It is presumed most people would agree with Faith's assessment there.

Faith yawned again.

She was supposed to be in at work today, writing some procedure for something dull. She offered to do it from the hospital bed but her company didn't want her to do that because that would be weird, they said. She kind of understood. Also...

She drifted off mid thought. Again, her dreams were meaningless. As were Michelle's.

^&*( )$%^*&($#%^*&(*)$*#(&

Jordan kept thinking about that night and giggling to himself. Sure, it would have been better if it [read: Faith] had died but, fuck, that was just perfect. Just as he hoped.

That bitch knocked him down, he called in the cavalry.

When he tried to congratulate the Kinzinger about the good shooting, the cop blew him off. But, yeah, that was just cover for sure. Who the fuck doesn't want to shoot some perverted trannies? What good white man doesn't?

Fuck, man, fuck. Yeah. This was good shit there, yeah. Good shit.

He wished he was there to see bitch's face as the bullet went in through that fat ass of hers. Yeah.

Really, though, great show. Jordan laughed at his own deed again.

He wished he would have kept the phone, but it was for the best he threw it off one of the bridges into the Rock River. It wasn't the biggest river but it would do. He took part of it and threw it off one bridge, the battery in another and another part off yet another. Very methodical. He was kind of proud of it. Because, honestly, he was evil.

Chapter 16

"All lives matter crowd didn't show up, did they?" Vannah asked, knowing the answer.

"Nope," Andrea said into the phone.

"Fucking cops. I'm sorry." A pause. "And your place?"

"I have 5 more days," Andrea said. "I gave him 400 dollars for another week and I got all my stuff in a storage unit."

"Did you tell her?"

"Who?"

"Faith," Vannah said. "Silly girl."

"No."

It's not often you can hear a disappointed look through a phone line, and yet this is what Andrea heard.

"You think I should," Andrea guessed.

"I think you should have. Now you have to soon."

"You know this is cliché lesbian shit, right?"

"Dear, you're getting evicted. The cops are gonna show up and, if you're lucky, they're not gonna shoot you, but just throw all your shit on the curb. Move in with her. You know she'll say yes. Her wife will too. Kind of have to, ya know?"

"It's not her fault."

"It's not her fault, no. But if she doesn't invite you to at least stay a while then you have an answer of what you are to her. And her wife. I mean, I think it's stupid what you're doing anyway, poly shit really does not work too much. But it's your call, honey."

"You're right."

"Of course I am."

"She'll be home in a few days."

"Lucky bitch"

"Yeah," Andrea said. "She was."

A pause.

"I was talking about you," Vannah said. "Gotta go."

^&*&^%$%^&*(#

Kinzinger got another message from that Jordan guy.

"Dude. Bad ass. Still laughing when I think about it."

He was up at 2AM and couldn't sleep. Administrative leave. Paid, of course. His union rep said it was completely normal and to not worry about it. Rest. Mandatory therapy.

Adam put down the phone. Dude didn't get it. Backseat cop. One of those. Not there. Not out there doing the things. You know?

What were the things?

He laid in bed for a while. Beside him was his wife. She was older, like he was. Stocky. Short. Didn't look much different from who he had shot. And for what purpose?

A tickle in his throat. A cough. The cat looked up and then put her head back on her paws and closed her eyes.

He was supposed to meet some of his friends—not cop friends specifically, but there were a few of them—at one of the outbuildings in Rock Cut state park. Not one of those ones off the lake but ones deep in the woods; they had been abandoned years before and left to rust, some administrator failing to allocate funds for demolition but, somehow, some still stood.

They went out there sometimes, these friends. They went out in the woods and talked about the world and how things should be. White, of course. Straight, of course. Christian, of course.

Though he had to change his phone number that had leaked somehow, his email was still what it was. He had gotten a couple other messages of support from his friends, either by shooting who he did or just even sympathy for the tough job, ya know, man, dude? But this Jordan guy was a little much. A little too far.

What was his deal? The Jordan fellow. He was going to be out there; he always was. He was like one of those nerds, though, that kind of was just humored by the older folks. He pushed things a bit. Like, they weren't Nazis, like he was, or claimed to be. Were they?

They humored him.

Reader, yes, yes they were. But they didn't see themselves as such. But just because they weren't tattooed with 1488 and swastikas and SS skulls and straight-armed salute doesn't mean they weren't the same damn thing. Just...different words. Different times. Same ideas. Same hate.

The unknowing Nazi eventually dozed next to his wife. He slept well, because, sadly and as a point against the existence of god, that is often what happens with bad men.

$%&^&*(&^%$#$^%*&(*(@

Andrea and Michelle were talking in the cafeteria. Faith was asleep upstairs and they had gone down to get some snacks. Andrea got some popcorn and pickles. Michelle got a yogurt.

They sat across from each other at a table. Just munching.

"Michelle?"

"Yeah."

Michelle looked at Andrea. Andrea looked down and kind of licked her lips for a second. What did she want? What was this about? Michelle felt very aware Andrea had asked her to join her for a snack all of a sudden. Was this planned? What was this?

"I..." Andrea started. Paused. Started again. "I'm getting evicted."

This was not what Michelle thought.

"Oh, sweetie is it money? We could lend you some."

"No no. I have money. Lucky. That's not it. The landlord wants me out because of the shooting thing."

"Oh. He can do that?"

"Yeah." Another pause. "I have most of my stuff in a storage unit. I just need a place to sleep until I can find another place on my own. Would you mind horribly if I stayed on your couch? I don't want to impose. And if you don't want I think I could arrange something else."

"No no. Did you ask Faith?"

Honestly Andrea had not had alone time with Faith since she was shot by Kinzinger. In the back. Yes. If that metaphor was not obvious.

"No. I figured it might be best to ask you first, independently of her."

"Why?"

"Because I am still unsure of where I stand with you? I don't know. I don't. This is stupid. Never mind. I'll just get a hotel—"

"Of course you can. We have a spare bedroom. It's not furnished; it's more of just a spare space that we toss stuff in but you can totally stay there for as long as you want. No couch. Home."

"You serious?"

"I wouldn't tell you if I didn't mean it."

Andrea smiled. Michelle reached over and put her hands on the table. Andrea put her hands in Michelle's. "No more shootings, got it?"

Andrea laughed. "Yeah."

Andrea started to pull away, but Michelle held her grip and continued. "I haven't felt safe in my house in months. I can't sleep. I'm tired. It saps my energy. Especially when I'm alone. I don't want to tell her not to see you because I can tell she is happier with you in her life." She stopped here, looked down, thought for a moment before continuing. "After my accident, I read a lot. Some religious stuff. Not a lot stuck but there was this concept in Buddhism they called it mudita. There's a couple other words for it; from my reading, poly folks call it compersion or frubble or whatever. Whatever. Words aren't things they're just pointers to ideas. Anyway, I derive joy from her joy. I am happy because she is happy."

"I get it."

"I hope so. I really do. But compersion can only sustain me for so long. I need her with me. And, well, if that helps her then I want you there, too. Not to mention having another person around might help me." A pause. A sniffle? Maybe, but Andrea couldn't tell. "I am glad to know you. I see what she likes in you. The way you talk to her in the room? So much nerd shit I can't stand it really but you two are both into it and I just feel infected by your..." she looked up at the sky, as if she would see the words in the ceiling. "Rapport? Passion? I don't know. Something like that. Just. I'm glad you're here. And I would be glad to have you under our roof."

%^&*(&^%$&^*&())

When Michelle and Andrea got up to Faith's floor, Faith could hear them laughing down the hall. Faith cringed for a second; was it a tinge of jealousy? Or just the stitches in her abdomen itching?

She tried to let it go and she felt it almost disappear.

They came into the room and Andrea was pushing Michelle in the wheelchair. Michelle did not like to be pushed by people she didn't trust. This was...this was good.

"Oh, she's awake," one of them said.

"Hi honey," the other one said.

They both came to either side of Faith and kissed her as they could.

"So," Michelle started. "Andrea told me she was in a pickle."

"Mmm. Pickles," Andrea said.

"Yeah, gross. What's with you two and pickles?" Michelle asked, shook her head. "Never mind. Anyway, she was saying she was needing a place to stay."

"Oh?" Faith asked. She really did not have a clue.

"Yeah, there was trouble at the apartment."

"Oh," Faith said and...kind of put it all together quickly without asking.

"So," Michelle said. "I told her she could stay at our place as long as she needed. It'll help you recover, it'll help me feel less alone, and she'll get a place to stay. We could always use help around the house."

Faith looked from her wife to her girlfriend and back again. This was a trap, of course. Wasn't it?

The trouble with paranoia is that it is ultimately narcissistic. Sometimes things were really what they appeared to be. Sometimes it was best, really, to just accept things at face value. Faith had not mastered this. She was under the impression they were speaking about her. About how she felt. About her needs and what would be best for her.

Andrea noticed the hesitation, the unexpected silence. "If it's okay," Andrea said. Her breath shallow in her lungs; Michelle also held hers tight.

Deep in her head, Faith's brain worked frantically, but of course it wasn't displayed. There was no real action there except kind of a blank stare for an uncomfortable couple seconds.

"Really?" Faith finally said. "Of course that's okay."

Andrea and Michelle both exhaled and giggled nervously, their mirror behavior leading to more laughter.

"Fuck girl, why do you got to scare us?"

"Because my brain sucks."

"But we both love your brain and you," Andrea said.

Faith and Michelle looked up. Andrea realized after a second what she had done.

Love. Fuck. What the fuck was that about? Did she mean it because she thought she should say that or did she mean it because she meant it? It was any of a billion things you could have said in response to the line that came before it; it's not like Faith said she had loved Andrea. She volunteered it first. So, she swallowed and admitted

"True though," Andrea said.

"Love you too, Andrea. And you, Michelle."

"Love you, too, Faith," Michelle said. Pause. A long one. Then, "You're okay, Andrea." She grinned and they laughed again.

Chapter 17

Adam Kinzinger sat in the grass of the state park, leaning back against an old and dead oak tree that had fallen in some storm. The park was huge, multiple lakes and ponds and rivers flowed through it, including I-90, a major interstate heading out of Chicago and through Rockford and on north to wherever, until it eventually curved toward Seattle.

But this was just the woods. A man leaning against a tree. Some men played music from a Bluetooth speaker with some rapper's name on it. This was a loose collection of men from various areas. They had met at Tea Party events and through police functions and through word of mouth. Did they have a name? No, no. They were not organized for a name. But they were of similar purposes, they had a certain feel for each of them. All of them, each and every one was white. They were all unqueer men. They were all older but not too old. They all were members of the NRA and other related, and in some cases, more extreme groups. Five of them were cops, not including Kinzinger, also there was a teacher and four skilled blue-collar workers. And, also, Jordan.

Adam didn't know what Jordan did for a living (because, to him, what else was there in life?). But Jordan was there, and occasionally he would look over at Adam from where he sat at some picnic table and give Adam a thumbs-up, his tattoos not baiting Kinzinger as much as that goddamned grin.

Completely fucking weird, ya know?

How did he insert himself? Adam didn't know. Jordan was here when Adam started hanging out with these guys.

Eventually Jordan came over and made himself comfortable next to Adam.

"Listen, dude. I don't want to talk about shooting that lady," Kinzinger said before Jordan could sit down.

"That was a man, dude. Besides, it was awesome."

"Whatever. I don't want to talk about it."

"I get it," Jordan said in a way that totally said that, no, he had absolutely no goddamned idea. "I'm just glad I called you in there that night."

Adam turned and looked at the kid. The man. This dude was a man. Just looked young. Caucasian. Thirty something? Male. Brown hair, blue eyes. wearing a camo top and jeans...Adam shook his head out of "identifying characteristics" mode.

"What did you say?"

"I thought you didn't want to talk about it," Jordan said because Jordan was, well, not terribly smart. A stupid grin on his face. His parents would have said "shit eatin'." If they talked that much.

"Did you call us that night on them?" Adam asked. A little louder, one of the others looked over and tapped in a buddy to watch.

"Yeah I mean. I was hoping you'd shoot the other one but, kill them all."

Adam grabbed the kid by his arm, some of the others started walking over. "The fuck is wrong with you, man?"

"Don't we want to kill all the faggots?"

"What's this 'we' shit?"

"You know, us. Gotta save the white race from inside and out. 14 words, right?"

Adam let him go and stood, then he bent over and pulled the tiny Jordan to his feet up again by the collar, one of the other cops arrived.

"What'd he do, Adam?"

"He called us that night. Couldn't take care of his shit on his own so he called us.”

“What night.”

“That night I shot her.”

“Him,” someone said, not Jordan.

“Whatever. This fucker called us.” Kinzinger pulled his collar tighter. “You knew there wasn’t anything. You knew.”

“I thought you would be cool with it. A chance to do your stuff.” Adam pulled him up again, closer to his face. He could smell Jordan’s shit breath. Literally smelled of shit.

“Let him go, Adam.”

“I want to beat the shit out of him.”

“That’s an order, Officer,” the other man said.

A second later, but one of those tense seconds seems like it goes on longer than it really does, he let go. “Fuck, man,” Adam said.

“He confessed?”

“Yeah.”

“Wait, confessed what?”

“To making a knowingly false call. Putting my life in danger. Almost killing someone.”

“Oh, come on that was a nobody faggot.”

“I don’t give a shit about them, you little fuck,” Kinzinger said, almost telling the truth, but brains being brains he was not all the way telling the truth. But mostly.

“I’ll take him, Kinzinger.”

“You sure, sarge?”

“Yeah. Yeah. Fucking A, man.”

“We could kill him,” someone said, though even if asked under oath nobody would say who. Especially the other men with “Protect and Serve” stenciled on their vehicles.

Sarge stopped.

Kinzinger said “He confessed to that or we charge him with it then they will have to admit there was nothing suspicious at the scene.”

“Kinzinger...”

"Yes, sir."

"Stop now. That's not how we do things."

Jordan said, "Yeah, you don't just kill people for no reason." The irony was lost on everyone present. Just that day, another black man was murdered on camera. So, as the astute reader would note, this is any other day in America.

"But he's nobody. Who would miss him? Why is he even here?"

"I thought he was with you," Sarge said to Kevin, one of the other cops. "No. I thought he was with Dave."

It went all around the group until they all realized Jordan was kind of liked by approximately nobody.

"We should be rid of him," Adam said and a small survey of the faces among them all showed nodding heads. "Nobody is going to miss him."

Sarge felt the weight of the pressure of his associates, the blue line circling in, wrapping about the whole group as they settled on what to do with this man and if the rule of law would be able to pierce that bubble and if, indeed, there would be blood.

&*(&^%*&*(_*&^%$%%*&^()_

Faith laid in bed mostly recovered. Obviously. Enough to go home, really. There is nothing more to be said here on that. No reason to draw out her recovery through another roommate whose church had demanded she carry her dead fetus, some complication occurring that robbed her of the ability to conceive again. Faith wept for the woman's lost fertility; it mixed with her own sadness.

"Should have been a mother, should have been a wife," she sang under her breath, crying. Nobody could hear her. She was alone. Michelle was driving to pick her up and Andrea was moving her stuff in.

Andrea was so confident in what she had chosen, her life and not having kids and the like. But sometimes Faith wanted to be a mother. She wanted to bear a child and hold it and feed it from her breast. None of these were possible. Michelle's doctor's recommended against it and they couldn't tell if that was some backwards-busted-ass thinking or some legitimate concern, so they heeded the advice. And, for a long time, another opinion was financially unattainable.

Whatever. She was waiting for the discharge nurse.

Just reminded of her feelings. Always reminded. Something around the corner reminded her always.

The nurse came in to give her some paperwork. A volunteer with a wheelchair came in after. They didn't want any patient to leave by walking, for some reason. So they pushed everyone out. Whatever.

"Good morning and happy release day! I'm Sylvia," she said. "I'll be escorting you out." She was an older Hispanic-looking lady with freckles covering her cheeks. "So hop on in."

As she was about to sit down a man in a suit knocked on the doorjamb.

"Pardon me. Faith Newbaure?"

"Yes."

"Do you have a moment?"

"And you are?"

"I'm Donovan Kastin, an attorney for the police department."

"I'm just leaving. Can this wait?"

He continued as if she said nothing. "I'm authorized to give you an offer to cover all your hospital expenses that were incurred as a result of the incident."

At least he ignored me like a man ignores a woman, Faith thought. She couldn't decide if she was offended or amused. She scrunched up her face and just said to the man, "Get out."

"Once I leave I do not think there will be another offer."

"Just go. The answer is no."

"Thank you. I am sure we'll see each other again," he said and then he was gone.

Faith and the volunteer shared a look. She said to Faith, "What a shit deal that would have been. Everyone knows what happened to you. Lucky lady. I mean, especially being white and all. Dropping charges. They would usually just have charged us with something. Lucky."

Faith sighed because she knew Sylvia was right.

"There was a cop here for a few days before you woke up. Watching you. Didn't see him?"

"No, I didn't."

"Usually that means they arrest you when you wake up but, you aren't getting treatment."

What could Faith say to that, really? That she should have? She was aware enough of the news. What could she do now? Sylvia broke the silence. "Sorry. It doesn't matter it is a good day for you. You get to go home. That is a good thing."

"Yes," she said. "It is."

Sylvia said, "Don't worry about the lawyers and the paperwork. Paperwork and lawyers always come."

$#$^&%*((#&^$%%^(&)&$^%*#(&^*%&$

Andrea was in her room. So weird she just had a room again. Like, not long ago: a whole apartment and not a tiny one either. But now she was in this room. This small-ish room would be big enough for a king sized bed and air. But she thankfully had a girlfriend who had a spare twin bed and a metamour who had some spare blankets and they united together for the goal of comfort.

Still wouldn't be able to fuck her in here. Well, maybe. It might be fun, holding onto each other for dear life as, well, you know.

So beyond the bed there was a desk with her computer setup she had at the apartment and a closet full of clothes stacked on the ground.

She crawled in her bed and started some music on her tablet that played from the speakers on the other side of the room. Then she picked up a book. Put the book down. She tried to sprawl out on her bed and stared at the ceiling; a fan with 4 blades pulled the air around, but the light was off; the sun poked through the curtains and left everything with a diffuse glow.

Did this feel like home? It certainly felt different. It was a place without neighbors sharing walls, except for the roof; that was only birds' feet and rain.

Laundry on-site. That was something. She wouldn't have to find quarters.

In a way, she kind of felt like she was back when she was little. Her room when she was a boy wasn't much different than this. She thought of herself, her childhood, as a boyhood. She had long reconciled that difference from the girlhood she ached for with what she had. And that boyhood, for her, was not all toxic and pain (though that existed), but filled with whatever it was.

But just a room like this? Not for a good long time.

But it was okay. These things were okay. She had her love here. They would sort out the sleeping things later. But here they were. Together. Under the same roof, as they say.

Andrea heard the keys in the front door and paused the music, then got up and went to meet the women she lived with and welcome one of them home.

~!%@#%$&(@$(&*)$

Jordan woke up covered in his own blood, sore and broken.

"Good. You're awake," Kinzinger said. "You don't fucking deserve to be but here we are."

"What do you mean?"

Kinzinger looked at the kid (because no matter how old he was, he still thought of him as a kid). "You have no idea, do you?"

"What?"

"I'm not what you think I am," Kinzinger said, not realizing he, indeed, was the thing Jordan thought he was. "I am not some hate filled person that just looks to shoot innocent people. I feel bad about what happened," he continued, and we can say with some confidence the last sentence there was true. "I wanted to protect people," Kinzinger lied, unintentionally. Again. The lies were repeated enough he just kept at them; it was kind of admirable in a sick, sad way.

"I became a cop to help people. I didn't want to go lording my power over someone," he continued, despite being exactly why he became a police officer. And, dear reader, one would be lying if one didn't guess most cops said the same thing but in their own ways were lying, too. Maybe to themselves. Because who really becomes a police officer, an agent of the state, with the oppressive systems and corrupt practices and even more corrupt people at the heart of those practices than someone who already knows, in their heart of heart, what they are: an aspiring tyrant.

Does the evil prince think he is evil? Of course not. He does things for the good of his people, as much as that works in his mind. But it is asinine and untrue, because sometimes those with power must acknowledge it is used for personal gain.

Something like that. I mean, the unconscious of Adam Kinzinger is both mysterious and hypocritical. But, as someone much wiser than your narrator said once, to live is to be a hypocrite. And Kinzinger certainly lived all he could.

"If you ever show your face around here, we will end you. Are we clear? You have two days to leave town and never come back," the cop said. "And that means calling us or those women or whatever they are again. You got it? You ruined my career."

But, dear reader, as I am sure you know, nothing happened meaningful happened to Kinzinger's career. It is not a spoiler to say he returned to work and really the only long-term consequence of his action was the occasional nightmare. And, eventually, those faded away too. The inertia of his career and life were too much to overcome because he simply shot a woman in the back.

$#^&%*^($%^&#$_+_+:'':{

Did Jordan leave?

One would suppose someone wouldn't go, but he was scared. Really scared. His perceived allies were not there for him, in fact, they were against him. Somehow? How did that work?

He packed up a few things. He lived with his mother because of course he did, but he told her he got a job with a friend roofing in Chicago. There was no job, but that's where he went.

That is the closure for Jordan.

No consequences. Not really. There were rarely consequences for men like Jordan. Did he ever realize what he was and what he had done and felt any remorse? It would be tempting to let him off with some spiritual awakening or the like, or to make karma kill him off, but neither happened. He just existed as a shell, for decades. He just existed.

Eventually he died. Something preventable, if statistical models hold, but why would he prevent anything? He just let it all go. No hope. No nothing.

His mother buried her son at 83. He left behind no heirs, no other mourners, and his funeral was attended merely by co-workers. And even they were few.

So when he finally did return to Rockford, it was in a box. And nobody objected in the slightest.

Chapter 18

Faith walked into her house and immediately smelled Andrea. Something about what lotion she used permeated the air already.

"Hi, honey," Andrea said, her arms wide.

"Hi!"

Michelle walked in on her crutches. "Hi, Andrea. Can you help get her bag from the van?"

"Sure," she said and waited for Michelle to pass and then ran outside barefoot.

Faith and Michelle looked at one another while they were alone for a minute.

"You ready to start this experiment?" Faith asked.

"I wouldn't have suggested it if I wasn't."

"I know. I just worry."

"I know."

"I love you, Michelle."

"Love you too," Michelle said. Andrea came in with a white plastic bag in her hand and another piece of luggage with some other junk in it. "Hell, now, I'm gonna sit down. You two make dinner. I'm gonna take advantage of this shit while I can."

The two women laughed. Michelle brought the items to Faith's room. Andrea and Faith made dinner together. Tacos. Because tacos rule.

Somewhere between the browning of the meat and preparing of the sides, all toppings *mise en placed*, Faith excused herself to use the restroom.

She peed. Just like she had done literally tens of thousands of times before. Then, while washing her hands, there was a feeling of whiplash, where Faith looked at herself in the mirror and see two images. Two. Two people where one person stood. Typically, it was no longer the possible girl sometimes showed up; she was usually there now, fully bloomed and manifest and real, but occasionally there was a man in the mirror. At this point, when she was feeling witty about it, he was the great [DEADNAME], slayer of hope, Faith's mother's son. And it didn't need to be related to anything going on in the world; the world could be perfect and then just, like, while brushing her teeth or washing her hand like this there would be this dude in place where Faith used to be.

And it hurt. It hurt so much and it sometimes even took her breath and put it in a bottle and there was nothing there to do but just try to breathe but the air wouldn't come. But she was breathing, of course, but instead of something slow and even it was fast, as if she had ran across the country and there was no air left in the world.

Sometimes the air would rush back in and she could feel relief. But it still left her exhausted and wanting to just lie down and let the suffocation take her. To let it all just end, to let the usage and abusage come and beat the ever-living-shit out of her. Lately, tears would sometimes come. Sometimes she was able to let the hold go and let the emotions come over every last goddamned inch of her brain.

Once the metaphors were mixed, it was hard to separate them. Can't un-fuck something. Can un-mix a metaphor without reworking the whole thing but in a way the whole thing not making sense and being all mixed up was part of the thing. *The thing the thing what was the thing?* She spent decades working and trying to work through what that thing was and how to express it and she made no fucking progress other than just there was a thing and it was this kind of mixed up thing she couldn't explain to a cis person if she tried and—

A knock at the bathroom door. Michelle spoke through the door. "You okay, hon?"

Had she been in there long?

"Yeah. Yeah. Just cleaning up a little. Spicy hands from the jalapeños."

"Okay. I gotta pee."

$%^&(*&^%$&^*&())(#*^%^%

In the kitchen, they sat around a table Faith had gotten from her grandparents. It was circular and so they were able to be equidistant from one another, with a good amount of room for elbows and forks and napkins and the like.

They were using no utensils because it was nachos and, well, the napkins were all the way over there.

About half-way through their first serving, over some light discussion of work-related venting, there was a ring at the doorbell.

Because Andrea still felt like a guest in the house, Faith got up first and went to the door. She looked out the window and saw a police car in the driveway, lights flashing. He was still in the car.

She opened the door.

It was the lawyer again. Donovan something? Kastin.

"Mr Newbaure."

"I'm not a mister."

"Forgive me. I am here to bring you this additional settlement offer—"

"We are eating dinner. You can call and speak to my attorney," Faith bluffed. She hadn't gotten one. That idea had seemed too distant and she was trying to just be normal again.

"Faith," the lawyer said. "We know you haven't retained counsel."

"What?"

"You don't have a lawyer. Listen, just take this. Don't sign it. Just take it and look at it and, if you find a lawyer, have him read it," he said, not registering the gender of lawyer he talked about, but Faith did. "You will find it is very generous." He passed her the paper; she took it.

He made a motion to tip his hat, even though he didn't wear one. He walked back to the cop car and the officer turned off the cherries and blueberries as Kastin got closer. He got in the car and they drove away, leaving Faith at the doorway, eventually joined by both her wife and girlfriend.

"That was fucking weird," Michelle said. "Can I see?" She held her hand out and Faith passed her the paper.

A dollar number written on the page was 6 digits, but the first one had a 1 in front of it.

Much thought would have to be done. They went back to the nachos and ate the rest of them in crunchy silence.

$%^&*()(*^%$%*^&(()

Dishes put away, television on showing random videos from YouTube, three adult women sat in a living room.

"The fucker interrupted dinner," Michelle said

"Yeah," Faith responded, looking blank.

Michelle and Andrea looked at Faith and then each other. Michelle chose another video.

After a while, Michelle said, "So where are you sleeping tonight, Faith?"

Faith's brain stopped thinking about the lawyer. This was a legitimate question. A gear shift, for sure, but a legitimate question.

"I," she started. Paused for a long time. Like, maybe she would not answer long time. "I don't know."

The other two women shrugged.

"Fucking A."

"I know, she gets two girls in her life and she can't decide who to fuck tonight."

"Oh, I know she's not fucking me," Michelle said. "Though cuddles are nice."

Andrea nodded. "Oh, for sure. You're gonna have to figure this out, Faith. I mean, either way is fine by me. I could totally rest," Andrea looked at Michelle and then again at Faith. This was planned, of course. To help her along to make her choose one way or the other, to decide, damnit. This, they both could sense, was not going how they thought. Faith had a distant look in her eyes Michelle couldn't identify but Andrea could without any trouble. Michelle noticed the hesitation but didn't put it all together. Just she missed that section of her brain, chronic self-doubt. The self-doubt was more like a muscle than a part of the brain, just chronic, ever present doubt. Michelle never had this. Andrea, though, knew. Blind spot.

"Hey, hon. You should be with your wife tonight. First day back after the hospital. I'm wiped from setting up my room. She's here and even just snuggling would be good I think. Do you? Want to snuggle on the couch? Or do you need to be alone?"

Too many questions. Too many, so many she froze again, her brain searching for silence or something quiet among all the noise, some pattern something to help her at the problem, whatever that was. Oh, was she losing where she was at that point? Where the world had lost all sense of reality?

Michelle was thinking about how she just wanted to hit Faith until she just fucking said something. Jesus. She sat there and did not move. Were these coming more since the killing? She couldn't remember before that.

Faith thought, break down the questions. But what were they again? She did know one thing.

"I don't know. I really don't. I just...just don't leave me alone."

()*&$^#%@%$^*&()_

That night, as Michelle and Faith lay in bed and watched TV, Michelle pulled herself up and laid her head on Faith's chest, just as she used to do. It hurt the growing and (second) pubescent tissue, but Faith let her because she missed holding her wife. Michelle's mind was quiet for now. And they were both quiet for a good long while.

Michelle touched the bandage.

"Hurt?"

Faith shook her head.

"I know you told me what happened. Did you think of anything when it happened?"

"Besides ouch?"

Michelle rolled her eyes almost hard enough for Faith to hear them.

"I...I don't remember, oddly. I don't. It was so quick and then I started to feel loose and not there. I...didn't do one of those near death things. I didn't see a light. Maybe I wasn't close to the end, but I wasn't scared either. Not enough time. Maybe an 'Oh no.' Which sounds totally lame or whatever."

Michelle grunted at *lame*. It was a word that bothered her. She was lame, after all.

"Sorry. You know what I meant." And that was the problem. Indeed Michelle did know, but Faith said it anyway.

"Yeah, go on."

"But just so fast. I don't even remember hearing the shot. I know I was on the ground. The guy had a gun out and pushed into my back and then...nothing."

"Weird."

"Yeah. You said you remember your back. And in a way I'm glad I don't remember. Mine sounds awful."

She did remember. She remembered the crack of a branch and then the crack of her back as she hit the ground and for a second it felt really nice, like cracking your back against a desk in school, where it went all the way up. As soon as it happened she tried to move; after that she felt nothing. Which, in a phrase, scared the ever-living-fucking-shit out of her. For a pretty good reason.

Faith made a sharp intake of breath. Michelle realized she was holding onto the bandage and tugging on it.

"What?"

"Sorry. Zoned out," Michelle said. "Sorry."

"It's okay. Sorry to bring it up."

"It's okay."

They laid together for a while, eventually Michelle pushed herself up and adjusted her legs on the bed. "Good night," she said to

Faith, puckering her lips a little.

"Love you."

"Love you, too."

"Good night."

"Night."

$%&^*&(*(&^%&$^*&(*(

Kinzinger sat in his living room. In his hand was cheap whisky in a tall glass, glass half-empty, two ice cubes half melted. The bottle open and on the counter in the kitchen.

He wondered if he should have planted something on the trans woman he shot in the back. He had a little pouch of pot to plant on people. They all did. It was almost standard issue.

The cop inside him wondered what he could get away with. Well, maybe not the cop inside. But the human inside him. Not all cops or some shit like that, right? He knew he fucked up and he was still wondering if he could get out of it. Admitting you fucked up to yourself is hard, he was finding. He kept searching his memory for a thing he could pounce on as proof he needed to shoot her.

If she had died it would have been easier.

That fucking Jordan guy, too. What did he say, between the punches? The sock full of quarters? Phone books were hard to find but they still had a couple lying about just for this particular task. Never trust a cop when their trunk contains a phone book for an area code a hundred miles away. But why would you ever be looking in the trunk of a cop car anyway? He called the cops because he got knocked down at a show? Can't even take care of his own fights. Calling in the cavalry for nothing and not even telling them what the fuck it was about.

His wife slept in the room above. He sat on the couch. He would sleep there.

He was wondering about his career and he had given no thought to the woman he had shot. And why would he? It's only human to think about how such things affected him. And, like most people, he was human, all too human. Still, he shot a girl and didn't care; he was half relieved she didn't die because manslaughter would be off the table, but he also knew it wouldn't be on because: the uniform.

It would almost have been better if she kicked it.

He swallowed a bit more whiskey. He tilted it back to finish it off and the ice hit his lip and the last bits flowed between the cubes. He parted his lips and let one enter. He crunched on it.

"Fuck," he said to the room. A kid was in her room (just off the living room) and she heard her daddy outside the room and she was sad to see and hear him so sad.

She didn't understand her father was evil and bad. He didn't understand it either; but neither of these saved him from fate.

Chapter 19

How many months does it take to fall in love? The subtle nascent love a partnership is built upon? Is it months? Weeks? And what about love that is not erotic? The love of friendship and respect, but is all. One would figure this would be faster, but it is not. Dear reader, do you love your friends?

As Andrea inserted herself into the flow of the household it became natural. With three people, there was an increased need to talk. Oh, Andrea had a work trip on the 22nd, so she'd be in Madison. Oh, Michelle was going to an appointment for dental cleaning on this day and Faith needed a follow up with the nephrologist. Dinner? Sure. Movies you want to see? Well, Faith wasn't interested in the Atomic Blonde movie (still too many guns on TV for her) so Andrea and Michelle went and they enjoyed it.

Blah blah blah.

Andrea and Faith snuggled on the couch while they watched movies. Sometimes Michelle leaned in.

^*(&)*&^%$&^*(

For months, the settlement contract sat on the counter, then attached with a magnet to the fridge. Nothing happened with it.

Faith sometimes looked at it. She looked up lawyers in her area. There were so many. Who to call? She quickly felt overwhelmed.

One time, her phone rang. She didn't recognize the number, but she answered it anyway.

"Faith? Donovan Kastin here. Have you given any more thought to the settlement? There is an expiration date on it."

She hung up on him.

She stared at the contract.

She Googled lawyers again. Felt overwhelmed.

She thought about her friends on the internet. Was there one? She lived in DeKalb. Still Illinois, right? Yeah.

What was her name? Taylor.

She Googled her. Dialed.

&*$#%^*&(*)(_&&$%^&*(

Michelle, eventually, started talking to guys again. This took months. But there was a dinner, then two; he was a new man was named Philip Alexie.

The first dinner they all had together was awkward. It would have been the third date but Michelle was a little freaked out by the idea of being alone with him. So she made it a double date. With Faith and Andrea.

"So, Philip, what do you do?"

"For a living? Well I am a—"

Faith cut him off. "No, what do you live for?"

Andrea laughed and Philip looked at her like there was something wrong with both of them. Andrea offered, "Long story."

"Well, that's an unusual question."

"We're an unusual family," Michelle said.

"I can see. Well, I live for literature."

"Oh. Cool. Who were your guys?" Michelle asked.

"Guys?"

"Yeah. Who do you read?"

"Right now I'm working on the latest Franzen," he said and Michelle's eyes almost rolled out of her head. "Oh, yeah, I know," he said. "But I kind go all over. Before it was some older stuff. I'd not read The Color Purple so I did," he said not quite realizing how it sounded to drop that book's title, "Then I went and read some of those classics we were supposed to read in High School and college. I mean like Moby Dick and other books by dead white guys. Apparently though I'm related to Cervantes somehow," he said and Michelle just kind of pursed her lips.

Philip sighed.

"I liked Moby Dick," Faith said.

"You never told me that before," Michelle said.

"You never asked. I mean, how many times does Melville come up in conversation?"

Michelle nodded at the point.

"My favorite was always Hemingway and Vonnegut." Andrea said. Almost shyly. "Hemingway was how I wanted to be...before. Vonnegut is just...it reminds me...it's...it's like an exhausted person telling the best story possible. So tired. Exasperated. I kind of feel that a lot."

Phillip and Andrea turned to Michelle, as if she would offer some literary guilty pleasure. Faith knew, of course. Michelle said, "I read only non-fiction."

"How can you only read non-fiction?" Philip asked.

"It doesn't interest me."

"And you haven't asked why other people do?"

"I presume it has to do with escapism. I mean, that's fine, just not for me."

Andrea said, "You watch TV with me."

"That's different."

"How so?"

"We're together," Michelle said, "doing something together."

"You never watched a TV show on your own?" Philip asked.

"I didn't say that."

"So?" Philip pushed.

Michelle adjusted herself in her chair. She felt an itch in her foot which sometimes manifested even though it wasn't possible.

There really wasn't much else to say on the subject. "I really don't care to talk about it.

Thankfully, (to everyone except Philip) the waitress brought appetizers, stopping part of the conversation.

When she left, Faith asked, "You know the poly thing, right?"

"Yeah," he answered.

"What do you think?"

"I honestly don't know. I've never done something like that before."

"Really? Well we haven't either."

"So how does it work?"

"We're still figuring it out," Andrea offered. They laughed

Michelle said, "Well you know Faith and I are married. But since her transition, she is a woman and all. And I am a straight lady."

"Poor girl," Faith said.

"Oh hush. She loves Andrea. And I really like Andrea too, but as a friend. We all live together, as you know." A pause, a quick look to see what volume of voice to use for some reason, "I don't have sex with them," she continued. "And you wouldn't with them."

Both trans women shook their heads, confirming no, indeed, there would be no three-some or more-some opportunities at the table. Was that hot? Was that what he hoped for? He had to admit, yes, that would be amazing. But he hadn't really counted on it. But, ya know, maybe a little.

^%(&*)_*&^%$^#&*(

"I must confess, Mrs Newbaure, I was hoping you would take our offer," Donovan Kastin said to Faith as they sat in an office in Faith's lawyer's office.

"Shut the fuck up, Donny," Faith's lawyer said. "You know as well as I do you wouldn't survive a court challenge. We've seen the video. She was lying still and officer Kinzinger shot her right in the back; there was no reason. The whole event was caught, context and all. You're lucky we're settling for this. Faith doesn't just want to be dragged through a trial and the media incurred."

Kastin shrugged. He had worked against Robin Taylor in the courtroom and she was competent. For a woman. He didn't say that of course. Just because he was a sexist asshole didn't mean he didn't realize he should just kind of flow with it for his client's best interest.

He just waved on the process. So, what were the terms? Well there was the cash: three million plus reimbursement for the medical bills. Not insignificant. What did they give up? Well, Kinzinger would have a job. Of course. No admitting wrongdoing.

They signed the papers.

He knew Taylor would get a chunk of change here. Maybe 500k. Which was fine, considering she worked, like, what? 10 hours on the case. Not a bad investment.

Whatever. Done. Move on. There were always other cases to file. Other things the cops would do. He couldn't clean up all their messes.

$%&^*&(*)(#$%^

The next day, when Michelle got the text said it was nice to meet her and her family, she realized Philip wasn't the one for her. She was a little upset. And by a little she was actually very very very upset.

She didn't say the words, but she thought them as she lay in bed alone that night; Faith had to head out of town for the day; she was not in Andrea's bed. She thought Faith was being selfish. That Faith ruined her life. That Faith wasn't really a girl. That Faith was the cause of all the problems. For a moment, she hoped the plane carrying her and 70 other innocent people would crash, killing everyone aboard. Or maybe the fuselage would be ripped off like happened over and over again when she was younger due to something mysterious called "metal fatigue" and it would pull her out somewhere over the Nebraska, slam her into the ground.

"Fuck I'm terrible."

She sighed. Almost cried for a moment. First about how she felt bad about her intrusive thoughts. Then about her situation. Her fucking useless legs as she leveraged them to turn on her side. The cries came and she was eventually weeping on her bed.

A knock on the door, tentative and scared as a knuckle tapping on a door can be.

Michelle took a quick second to dry her eyes, "Yeah?"

"You okay?" Andrea said through the door. "Do you need anything?"

"Open it," Michelle said.

"I heard you crying. You okay?"

"Yeah," Michelle said. "No."

"Do you want to talk?"

"No. I just...you can sit down."

Andrea came in and sat on the far corner of the bed.

"What's up?"

"Just frustrated."

"At?"

"Men."

"Oh."

"Like, did I roll a worse hand? I mean, in a poly with a trans woman and her partner but no threesomes, disabled, and being everything else. Why is it so hard?"

Andrea didn't know and hesitated. "I don't know," she eventually said.

"I am not asking for fair, I'm just asking for a chance, ya know?"

"I know."

"And I don't even get that far."

"Did you date before?"

"Before?"

"You met Faith?"

"Oh. No. You know."

"It was a while ago."

"I know."

"Dating is different now," Andrea said. "Before I found Faith I was seeing ladies and even guys because I was just desperate. Online, ya know. Easy come easy go."

"And how did you find Faith?"

"Dumb luck," Andrea said. "Just, she's...nice. So nice. Everything like that is dumb luck. Like, in the original sense of the word 'dumb'."

Michelle had the true there.

"I ever tell you what she did that first night?" Andrea asked.

"No."

"She put a blanket on me. After I fell asleep on my own couch."

Michelle smiled. It was just like Faith to do that.

"You found her. You'll find another caring person. We'll help you. But you just have to keep throwing yourself out there. All over. It's what people do now. It's weird but yeah, that's what it is." Andrea looked down and found a blanket, picked it up, then continued, "the good people in your life will help you become a better person yourself." She stood and gave the blanket to Michelle.

"You're a good woman, Michelle. We'll find someone for you. And until then, we'll maybe find some someone to have fun with. It's not as if you have to marry the person you just met." Something about the voice then when Andrea said "marry." Michelle picked it up. The hesitation of the word, did it mean anything? She would see. Andrea soldiered on, "For now it's just good to have fun."

"Okay."

"You should have fun. You deserve it."

Michelle wondered if she did, really. Even as Andrea gave her a hug. Even as Andrea walked out. As she closed the door. Michelle wondered if she deserved to be loved because she wasn't enough, because she wasn't enough to stretch and be everything she could for Faith.

It was just sex, right? It shouldn't be important.

But she knew better. It was. She just couldn't. She conjured the images of Faith on her, going down on her, doing things. It felt wrong. Not bad just incorrect. She put Andrea in place, for thought experiment purposes, and the same.

Philip though. That was right.

Though not him, precisely.

She missed being touched. Though that was as much on her as anyone; well, as much as this whole fucking biological lotto is on anyone. She struggled, but she knew she was just a little unluckier.

Fuck. "I hate being straight."

Maybe cuddles? Michelle struggled to find a place to be okay with that. Failed.

Reader, I am sure we all wish it was something she could change. She had tried. After Faith came out to her, Michelle tried to "mess around" with her, but it always felt weird. Faith smelled different now. Her skin was softer now. Her face was rounder now. Her breasts had come in slightly and it was weird to suckle them like Faith loved.

She pulled her legs to flip over and silently swore but she did feel better, a little. Andrea was right. Intellectually she knew it. Even if the emotions were a little hard to put down and sort.

She re-thought the conversation, but got stuck when Andrea said the word "marry." She had hesitated. Something, somewhere clicked in her head Andrea was going to ask Faith to marry her.

It wouldn't be legal. Polyamorous relationships like theirs were bad for the state apparently, but there was a symbolic act there. It was beautiful in its way. But was it too quick? Was it too soon? I mean, how long had it been? Michelle couldn't remember, but she knew how much they had done. Oh, of course she remembered when it started, but it hardly seemed like it had been that long, even though she remembered how it felt to kill man.

Would she ever tell a date that? She didn't know.

Oh god. How was she going to ask? Was she going to marry Faith?

How did she feel about it? She pondered the smiles on Faith's face, and the occasional soreness of her own cheeks in laughter and joy. The way an extra pair of hands helped. How there was an opportunity for solitude regularly made Michelle happy.

But Faith. Oh god, had she ever been happier?

"Andrea!?" she called out.

A few seconds later the squeaks outside the door stopped and the doorknob turned.

"Yeah?"

"You're going to ask her marry you, aren't you?"

Andrea stared at Michelle. How the fuck did she know? How? "How?"

"Guessed."

Andrea stood there with her jaw a little open.

"Yes," she said. Nervous. What would both woman say? was a big step.

Michelle squealed with joy and hit her hands on the bed. "Oooh yes! That's so amazing." She threw her legs onto the ground and with the practice decades of having no control over her legs, she leveraged herself up to stand shakily, one hand on a wall to steady her.

"Congratulations! Now hug me and help me down. This isn't as easy as I make it look."

Andrea ran forward and embraced her girlfriend's wife and held her tight, even kissed her cheek. Surprised "Thank you"s were whispered into Michelle's ear, nobody quite sure why her voice was small.

"Oh, it's not up to just me. You have to ask her too."

$^&(*)_*)&%^$&(*)

Faith didn't know how to react when Andrea opened the car door for her.

"This is a special evening. We've been together for a year now. And I wanted to treat you right."

"Well thank you," Faith said, completely unsure what the hell was going on.

The restaurant was mostly empty. The dark lighting let everyone inside feel as if they were alone, but they were not. It wasn't a big place. It was downtown and nestled near some art galleries and some hipster Absinthe bar. Not far from Andrea's old loft. An attempt to gentrify, some would say. But that was how it was. There are no idyllic and pure places.

The wine was white and the appetizer was light.

Andrea held the small box with her hand in her purse. Her other hand was in Faith's.

"I love you," they each said.

Should this be before the entrée or after? And why didn't she think of it or google it before? She couldn't remember.

Fuck!

The entrées arrived. She dropped the box back into her purse. They ate. They talked. They held hands. They spoke vaguely of the future, of the possibility of children and of growing old.

As the dishes were cleared and dessert contemplated, Andrea figured this was the moment.

She rose as if she was going to the rest room, but instead stopped and turned and dropped to her knee. Faith sat utterly still and unsure what in the world was happening. It felt surreal and not wrong but improbable, as if this were some dream but...

"Faith, you have blessed this woman with a love more pure than I could imagine. You have given me hope and happiness and a home and for all these things I am forever grateful and humbled you would share them with me. I ask you the only way I know how, to commit myself to you in love. Faith Newbaure, will you marry me?" Andrea opened the box, in the box was a ring, of course, with red rubies and dark onyx stones and in the center a simple gem; was it diamond? She couldn't tell (it was, but human made, as ethical as consumption under capitalism could be, the narrator supposes).

Faith brought her hands to her mouth and looked at Andrea.

"But..."

Andrea produced from under the box a small square piece of paper, she handed it to Faith, who unfolded it.

"Faith. Say yes. —Michelle."

And so she did. "Yes. Yes. A thousand times yes!"

Chapter 20

There are forty-four thousand of some odd things to do before a wedding, and Andrea and Faith's was more of the same. The cake, the officiant, the catering, the DJ, the bar, the guest list, the vows, the dresses, the venue for the ceremony and the one for the pictures and the one for the reception, the makeup, the hair dresser for both of them, the colors to coordinate, the bides maids and the grooms- men and what to call the enbies who wouldn't be either [companion, brides' friend, matrimonial assistant, brides mate?], the music and the photographer, the menu, the diet needs, the children policy, the flowers, and the way to explain this was a poly thing, the way to explain Michelle wasn't going anywhere, the honeymoon, the role Michelle would have, the role her new boyfriend would have, the everything else...*your narrator gestures at world*

And that was all if everything went smoothly. Even if they didn't have to go through two florists and three cake people to find some- one who would cover their poly tranny wedding or whatever the fuck it was, they said. They could have sued and maybe even talked to a lawyer but there was a not insignificant expense.

When it was done, when it was all done, there was still so much to do. Would there be a honeymoon? Days off work prepared, pass- ports required, plane tickets booked or hotels or other accommoda- tions of some sort. Were the places they were heading safe? Would they be able to do the sights?

But at last came the day. That day neither of them expected would ever happen. Where they stood in their wedding dresses in front of their friends and family. Vannah and Michelle and Marc and Jessica there, an enby named Mitch being a bride's mate behind Faith, and a coworker of Andrea standing there, completely all confused amongst the throng of queer friends and relationships.

Two women stood before them all and said their vows. They were not in a church or any place of worship, but they stood in front of a lake and among the trees and

"To have and to hold."

The vows were traditional

"In sickness and in health."

Not because they were traditionalists

"For richer, for poorer."

But because the vows were right for them.

"I now pronounce you," the celebrant said, "Wife and wife. You may now kiss the bride."

^*&()_*&^%$#$^*%&()()

That night, in the hotel room, they made love. They touched each other and held one another and their scars were not remains of battle zones but signposts of lives and experiences lived and where they each came from and each were maybe going.

Faith's scars were still fresh, the shiny skin from the wound on her stomach and back touchy.

Andrea held her close, kissed her, their soft lips and tongues touching, their hands holding one another, mouth on mouth and mouth on breast and mouths and hands on each other's girldicks and they each held the other close.

They made love, their hair in the other's face, the awkward grunts and sounds and words and mumbled requests and screams of joy and the way their bodies responded now estrogen ran through their systems. Kisses on necks and hickies and scratches and rubbing. Once, Andrea got a cramp in her leg and Faith helped massage it out and kissed it better and then started kissing up her thigh and buried herself in Andrea's belly and blew air onto it to make noises like farts in there and that made them both laugh.

They spent the night and morning with one another as they would for many more years. Michelle would be there, too. She would find a man, eventually, but it was hard for her, but he was good when she found him, and even ever after.

One time they talked about children. About adopting a queer teenager. They never did, not for malice or spite or anything of the sort but just because it never happened.

Another time, they all took a vacation to an island off the coast of some other island. It was perfect and they sat on the beach.

To have and to hold.

And when Michelle married her boyfriend, Andrea and Faith were there, too. When he moved in and they quickly discovered they needed to find a bigger place for four adults and a rather large dog.

There are endings where there is nothing but death and hatred and evil and those are deep and literary endings. But sometimes there are good endings. Where the girl gets the girl and they live happily ever after or at least something close enough to can be called that. There are endings were the world ends and some where the world moves on and some where they start where they begin.

This is one of the happy endings, where our Faith and Andrea and Michelle all live. Where Vannah moves back nearby and they all find good jobs but Marc, dear Marc, does die. A motorcycle accident. Years later. He should not have been drinking. This is the tarnish on the full glass on the happiest of endings.

But reader, dearest reader, if you remember Andrea and Faith, remember them as their wedding photos showed them, two brides, dressed in white, holding hands and kissing one another, a crowd out of focus behind them, the love strong against the world who would split them, true to one another, good and pure as can be.

Thanks

I started writing this novel in April of 2017. It started with just the title. Since then I have been supported by hundreds of people—if not thousands—in various ways. I regret that my memory is poor and this will only serve as an example thereof. Thank you to my wife and children. Thank you to Kate, Jenny, and Siobhan; these three ladies believed in me when I didn't. Thank you Julie and Mitch and Sydney, you are all loved. Thank you Robert and Christina; Marcos and Willie Mae; Dillon and Irena, Josh, Dina; Krystal, Patrick, Krystal, Bethe, and Caleb and Ryan; Dylan, Ashely, and Angela too. Thanks Kristin, Nicole, Callen, Vannah, Rachel, Maddie, Kelley, Jessica, Bryon, Markie, David, Meg, Wynne, Melissa, Kiva M and Raine, Chroma, Cass, Kiva B, Gin, Eva, Tegan, Mari, Yael, Rose, Serene: you all helped me in various ways I am unlikely to completely explain coherently. Thank you to those who read drafts (Jenny, Mitch, Sydney, Mary, Sandra, various others) and gave valuable feedback, though all errors are mine and mine alone.

Thank you to those trans authors, artists, performers, musicians, and others who have come before. Your voice was heard and appreciated and loved.

Thank you to Madison and HYBRID Ink for this opportunity.

If I have forgotten your name, I am sorry but no less grateful.

About the author

Jen Durbent is a poet, writer, and stand-up comedian who grew up in and is based out of the greater Chicagoland area. She lives with her wife, children, three cats, and a very old dog. She uses "she," "they," or "it" pronouns.

She can be found on the web at jendurbent.com or Twitter as @JenDurbent. *My Dinner with Andrea* is her debut novel.

About the publisher

HYBRID Ink, LLC began in 2018 with this, it's inaugural publication. Borne out of a desire to see more of the publications they loved, Madison Scott-Clary and the editors at HYBRID Ink made it their goal to provide well-versed and sophisticated works of fiction, poetry, and creative non-fiction.

We want writing that gets us thinking about ourselves, stories that span genres, and words that change the way we look at the world.